Love You Always

A Brother's Best Friend Small Town Romance

AJ Alexander

LOVE YOU ALWAYS by AJ Alexander
www.authorajalexander.com
aj@authorajalexander.com

First Paperback Publication: September 2024
Photo provided by: Wander Aguiar
Cover Designer: Wildheart Graphics
Developmental Editing: Made Me Blush Books
Line Editor: The Ryter's Proof Editing Services
Proofreader: Crystal Clear Author Services

dedication

To everyone who never felt worthy.
You are loved. You are worthy. You are enough.

prologue

emersyn

"Great party, Em!" Sophie shouts into my ear over the loud music.

I nod my head, not even bothering to respond as we walk through the front door of my parents' house. I look around the room, searching for my only reason for coming tonight. I'm not a party person, much to my best friend Sophie's chagrin, but tonight, I've made an exception.

"I wonder when Brady will get here." She winks at me. "I'm going to grab a drink. Do you want anything?"

It takes my brain a moment to process that she's even asked me a question, which causes my cheeks to heat in embarrassment. "Sure. Whatever you're having."

"Girl, you need to relax. Everything is going to work out." Sophie giggles, giving my hand a tight squeeze.

"I wish I was as confident as you," I whisper, as my

eyes continue to scan the room, searching for wavy golden-brown hair among the guests.

My heart constricts in my chest as I think about what I plan to do tonight. I'm terrified of what might happen and how things could change for the worse, but I can't keep hiding. At this point, it's now or never.

"I can be confident enough for the both of us." She gives my hand one more squeeze before weaving her way through the bodies toward the kitchen, and then I turn my attention back to the dance floor.

My brother, Beckett, can throw one hell of a party. He never needs a reason, but today's party is important. It's more of a going away party than a celebration, but it's not like this is the first time his best friend has left on deployment.

Brady Thomas and Beckett have been thick as thieves for my entire life. Where one went, the other would soon follow. That is, until Brady joined the Marines right after their high school graduation. That was one place Beckett wasn't going to follow his best friend. Instead, Beckett decided to stay here in town, buying a bar down near the waterfront. Even though their paths have diverged, the two of them have remained as close as brothers. Even our families are close. We spend most holidays at each other's houses and even take summer vacations together.

"I'm sure lover boy will show up soon." Sophie bumps my shoulder before handing me a red Solo cup.

I sniff the cup, then hold it out at arm's length. "Beckett is going to lose his shit if he catches me with this."

I shove the cup toward her, not wanting to get on my brother's bad side. The term *overprotective brother* was created for Beckett Carter. When he was about twelve years old, after his mom passed away, our parents got married, and I followed a little more than five years later. Mom says that when he saw me for the first time, he told our parents he would do anything to protect me, but as we grew older, something changed. It's like he woke up one morning and decided it was his mission in life to protect me from anyone with a penis—especially Brady. I was worried for a while that he somehow got wind of my massive crush on Brady, but Beckett isn't someone who keeps his opinions to himself. If he'd known and had a problem with it, he would've said something. I wouldn't have listened to him, but I digress.

On the one hand, I get it. I'm the little sister he swore to protect from the world, but I'm no longer the baby girl our parents brought home from the hospital. Someone who can't make her own decisions or think for herself. I love my brother, but if he doesn't give me some space, I'm going to lose it.

"Beckett won't know if you don't tell him." Sophie's voice brings me back to the present as she takes a healthy pull from her cup. "It's only a few weeks early.

Besides, you need to lighten up if you're going to make your big confession to Brady."

You would think that being the source of much small-town gossip when we were younger, Sophie would be a little less...well, her. She's always danced to her own beat, not being one to follow the rules that society has set out for us. With the bright blue streaks in her blonde hair and tattoos covering both her arms, you'd expect a rebel, someone who hates to follow the rules, but what you get is the most loyal person you will ever meet. She has an amazing dad, who raised her all on his own, respects her need for self-expression, and wants nothing more than for her to be happy in everything that she does.

Sophie and I met on our first day of kindergarten. Her mom had just taken off, and her dad, Mr. King, had just moved them back to Tyson's Creek from Atlanta, to be closer to family. She made a beeline for me the moment our teacher told us to choose our seats and declared we'd be best friends for life. And she was right. Hence why she is the only person who knows about my feelings for Brady.

"Will you keep your voice down?" I whisper loudly, my cheeks instantly heating in embarrassment.

Sophie giggles softly as she takes a sip from her cup, her eyes scanning the room over my shoulder. "And the devil appears."

I spin around and freeze as I find Brady striding

through the front door. His long, lean legs are covered in painted-on black jeans, and a black leather jacket hangs off his broad shoulders over a tight-fitting white T-shirt. My gaze continues up his body before locking eyes with him. A devious smile covers his face as he throws me a wink.

I lower my head before taking a nervous sip from my glass. I've been in love with Brady Thomas since I was old enough to know what love was. He was the first boy to tell me I was beautiful, even though we both knew he was lying through his teeth. He was my first date, taking me to my junior prom when no one asked me. Brady was my personal knight in shining armor.

"Busted." Sophie giggles. "Now, who's the gorgeous man who came with him?"

"I thought you only had eyes for my brother?" I tease, peeking toward the door at Brady for a second time.

Sophie has had a massive crush on my brother for just as long, if not longer, than I've had mine on Brady. I doubt Beckett has any interest in my friend, but she refuses to give up hope, claiming she'll wear him down eventually. I love her optimism, but I don't think anything will get my big brother to notice her. Not even her tattoos, piercings running up both of her ears and one in her nose, and brightly colored hair.

"That's one of Brady's military buddies." I pause

for a moment, trying to remember his name. "I think his name is Seth, but I'm not sure."

"Whatever his name is, he's the perfect person to help make your brother jealous." Sophie smiles brightly in my direction, but her face falls.

I turn, following her line of sight, and catch a glimpse of Bristol and Seth huddled together near the makeshift bar. I shake my head, throwing my arm over my friend's shoulder.

"Maybe next time you should clue Seth in to your master plan." I smirk at Sophie as she crosses her arms over her chest.

"All the good ones are unavailable," she says longingly as my brother strolls into the room toward Brady.

I freeze. A woman with blonde hair, who seems vaguely familiar, squeals in delight as Brady lifts her in the air and twirls her around before planting a kiss on her lips. The cup I'm holding slips through my fingers, crashing to the floor and spraying beer across my legs.

"That could be anyone." Sophie grasps both my hands, turning me toward her. "Take a deep breath and think things through."

Pain like I've never imagined slices through my chest as my heart cracks open. I'm not naïve. Brady is gorgeous, turning every single woman's head whenever he walks into the room. At thirty-seven, I doubt he's been living as a monk, but this is the first time I've seen it right in front of my face.

"It's Leia." Sophia squeezes my arm as she points toward the group in question.

"Are you sure?" I croak, fighting to hold back the tears threatening to spill from my eyes.

"Judging by the way Riggs just ripped her from Brady's arms and planted himself between them, I'm 100 percent sure that's Leia."

I blink, attempting to clear my vision as I focus on the group around Brady. The scene looks just as Sophie described. Riggs has positioned himself between Brady and Leia, shielding her from his view, as Leia tries and fails to step around him before giving up with a huff.

"When are those two going to just get it on already?" Sophie giggles, taking another pull from her cup.

"About the same time Beckett professes his undying love for you," I deadpan, rubbing at the spot over my heart.

"Soon, then."

"Sure, whatever you say," I mumble, my attention still focused on the group standing around Brady.

Beckett is flanking Brady, his arm lazily resting on his shoulder as they both talk with the blonde-haired woman, Riggs Monroe, and Leia's older brother, Walker. I don't know either of the guys very well, since they both live in a different town, but I have seen them hanging around Crawdaddy's whenever Brady is in town.

Walker is a bear of a man, towering over Leia, which makes her look more like a toddler standing next to him. His dark brown hair is styled perfectly to give it that just-out-of-bed look without being too messy. His cerulean blue eyes shine brightly as he throws his head back and laughs at something Brady says.

Riggs's posture is still tense, his eyes flicking between Brady and Leia as if he's assessing a threat. Is Brady a threat to whatever is going on between Riggs and Leia? I mean, she wouldn't have thrown herself at him the moment he walked through the door if he wasn't, right? Or was she doing it to make Riggs jealous? Is that even something she'd do? My mind races with all these questions, trying to make sense of what I saw and know to be true, but I'm failing miserably.

"I'm going to go get some fresh air," I murmur, needing to put some space between me and Brady for a few moments.

"Want me to come with you?"

"Nah. I'm good," I respond before pulling from her grasp. I weave my way through the crowd and then slide the back door open and step into the cool night. Pulling my sweater tightly around my body, I wrap my arms around my waist before tilting my chin toward the sky and blinking rapidly.

"What the heck is going on with me?" I say to myself, the urge to cry slowly dissipating. "He isn't mine."

"Who isn't yours?"

I spin around and lock eyes with Brady. *What the hell is he doing out here?*

"Is some guy giving you a hard time?" he asks, pulling his arms out of his jacket and draping it over my shoulders. "I can go knock him around a little for you."

I giggle softly. "No, he's kind of dense." I pull the sleeves of his jacket over my hands. "Besides, it's not his fault. I doubt he even knows I exist."

How ironic. I wonder how different the conversation would be if he knew that the man who sent me running from the party was him.

"I doubt that." Brady's eyes soften as he pulls me into his chest, burying his nose in my curly dark brown hair.

"It's you," I whisper as I wrap my arms around his waist, squeezing him tightly and hiding my face in his chest.

"What about me?" He pulls back slightly, tucking a few loose strands of hair behind my ear.

"Nothing. Forget I said anything." I drop my head and try to pull out of his arms, but his hand tightens along my waist.

Brady grips my chin between his thumb and index finger, lifting it slowly. His forest-green eyes stare down at me, searching for the answer to his question.

"Em, you can tell me." His eyes swirl with adoration and something else, something that I've never noticed before.

It can't be. There's no way.

I shake my head to clear my thoughts. "Not this, Brady."

"Yes, this," he pleads. "Tell me."

I close my eyes tightly, unable to deny his request but not knowing how to begin. How do you tell someone that you long to be with them? That they are the air you breathe and the heartbeat deep inside your chest. That you have no idea when it happened, but you can't bear to spend one more day without letting them know how you feel. How deeply and irrevocably in love you are with them.

I open my mouth to respond but clamp it shut tightly. Panic swells in my chest at the idea of him not feeling the same way for me. Of ruining whatever this tentative friendship is between us. I love Brady. I will always love him, but is it better just to keep things the way they are now? No. I can't do that. Not now. Not with him leaving with a chance that he'll never be back. I don't want to live my life with regrets, wondering how things could've been if I had been brave enough to tell him how I felt about him.

"Brady," I whisper as I rise onto my toes and wrap my arms around his neck before leaning forward. My lips brush against his once before I pull back and gather my courage. "I love you."

His eyes darken as a low rumble escapes his throat. Then, before I can react, he leans down, crashing his lips into mine. We both groan as Brady nibbles and sucks at my bottom lip before running his tongue along it.

"Emersyn," he groans as he threads his hand in my hair, gripping the coarse hairs near my scalp tightly and pulling my head back to get a better angle, possessing me in a way I never imagined was possible.

Every nerve ending in my body sizzles with anticipation as his hands slide down my body, cupping my ass. I want to give him everything in this moment—everything that I am now, everything that already belongs to him.

We break apart, gasping for air, and he pulls me closer to him and nibbles down my neck.

"I've dreamed of this for years," he whispers against the soft skin of my neck before brushing his lips softly against mine. "But I never believed..."

"What in the fuck is going on out here?" Beckett bellows as he slams the back door shut hard behind him. "I come out here to check on my baby sister, and I find my best friend molesting her!"

"Beckett, don't be so dramatic." I roll my eyes, resting my head against Brady's chest.

But instead of feeling his strong arms wrap around me, holding me tightly to him, I feel his entire body stiffen.

"Emersyn, go inside," my brother growls as he inches his way toward Brady.

Beckett's hands open and close tightly, his muscles rippling as he fights to keep control of his anger. Brady pushes me behind him, but I know that no matter how angry he is, Beckett will never hurt me.

"I'm not a little girl, Becks," I growl as I step between the two of them, using my brother's most hated nickname to prove a point.

"Go inside, Emersyn," Brady says softly, giving my hand a squeeze. "I promise we won't do anything but talk."

Beckett growls as Brady kisses my forehead, then he grabs my hand and pulls me toward him and away from Brady.

"I'm not a toy for you to fight over, Becks." I snatch my hand from his grasp. "I love you, but if this is how you are going to act, then I have nothing to say to you."

I take one more look at Brady over my shoulder, and he smiles gently at me, assuring me that everything will be okay.

"Don't beat him up too bad," I say to Brady and sigh. "I don't think Uncle Sam will take too kindly to having to bail you out the night before deployment."

"I make no promises." Brady winks before turning his attention toward my brother. "We'll be inside in a few minutes."

I turn without another word and head inside.

one

brady

six months later

"When is she going to stop emailing me?" I mumble to myself as I notice another email from Emersyn.

Emersyn Carter has been the star of all my fantasies for the last three years. I've known Emersyn for her entire life, but when I came home on leave after being deployed, she wasn't the same little girl who kissed my cheek and begged me to come home safely. I walked into their parents' house expecting to find the same little girl I've watched grow up over all these years, but instead, I was brought to my knees. Gone was the little girl I'd once known, and in her place was the woman of my dreams.

My heart lurched in my chest like my body finally recognized her as its other half. The only problem is she's my best friend's little sister. I tried for months to remind myself that she was just Beckett's annoying kid sister, but it quickly became impossible. I was finally seeing her for who she really was: an intelligent, gorgeous woman who was too good for me. But no matter how hard I tried, I couldn't forget her. I yearned to be near her, to spend as much time as I could with her when I was home on leave. I even found myself making excuses to come home on leave, hoping for the chance to see her. Now that the wool has been removed from my eyes, there is no denying how much she means to me.

I'd like to think that Beckett had no idea about my sudden infatuation with his sister, but that'd be a lie. He must have noticed something had changed between Emersyn and me because he became overprotective, doing anything and everything he could do to come between Emersyn and me. Each time I made an excuse about wanting to drop in and see his mom or asked if his sister was home visiting from school, I gave him all the more reason to try and put as much space between me and his baby sister. About a year after I realized my feelings for Emersyn, he told me in no certain terms that I wasn't good enough for his sister, not that I didn't already know that.

My life was going nowhere before I enlisted in the Marines. When we graduated from high school, everyone else had a plan for what they were going to do after graduation, but I had nothing. No prospect for a job, no plans to go to college, nothing. I figured something would fall into my lap or I'd come across something that I'd know deep in my soul was what I was supposed to spend the rest of my life doing. And I found that the day I saw a few Marines in uniform having coffee in front of Just the Drip. One of them caught my attention and asked me if I wanted to join them, and the rest is history. I went home and told my parents I was enlisting right after graduation.

Beckett made sure I understood that even though we were friends, he wasn't handing Emersyn over to me with his blessing and best wishes for our happiness. Beckett never understood my decision to join the Marines. He never outright said it, but I think a part of him thought we would both stay here and run Crawdaddy's together. Not that the idea wasn't tempting, but I felt that giving my life for my country was something I was called to do.

So, to Beckett, I was a Marine. Someone who couldn't guarantee that they would come home at night. Emersyn had her entire life ahead of her, and there was no way he was going to stand by and allow her to be hurt like that. I knew he was right. Now, not only was I not good enough for his baby sister, but I was going to die and leave her heartbroken, and that got to me.

There was no way I could guarantee that I would make it home after every deployment, but this was going to be the last one. I'd never have to leave Tyson's Creek or her again. I naïvely assumed that Beckett would understand. Sure, he wouldn't give his blessing right away, but we'd known each other for years. He knew me and knew I'd never hurt his sister. Too bad things didn't go as planned.

Memories of my going away party—the last time I saw Emersyn—filter through my mind. The way the light reflected off her tear-stained cheeks as I cupped her face in my hands. The smell of honey and lilac wafting off her skin as I pulled her in for a kiss. The way her lips tasted slightly bitter, like cheap beer and something sweet as I pulled them between mine and claimed her mouth as my own. My entire world tilted on its axis when she told me she loved me, but then I let my best friend's words ruin everything.

"What the fuck were you doing out here with my sister?" Beckett shoves me hard in the chest, causing me to stumble back slightly. His fists clench at his side, like he's trying to hold himself back from punching me.

"What did it look like I was doing?" I cross my arms over my chest, not wanting to lash out at him. "Why do you seem so surprised, Beckett? You've been doing everything in your power to keep me away from your sister."

Probably not the best thing to say to him right now, but he doesn't deny it. Beckett has always been overprotective of Emersyn. I would be, too, if I had a gorgeous little sister like her, but I'm the last person he needs to protect her from.

"Trying and failing, it seems," he mumbles as he

strides past me toward the table in the opposite corner of the small patio, bumping my shoulder hard.

"There's no need for this macho bullshit, Beckett. Say your piece, but we both know my feelings for Emersyn aren't anything new."

He scoffs before pulling out a chair and taking a seat, resting his ankle on his knee. "Yes. You've been in love with each other for years, but that doesn't mean I have to like it."

Both? It seems my friend has been keeping things from me, but why?

"You knew and said nothing? Why? Why would you stand between us when you knew how much I loved her? You know I'd do everything in my power to make Emersyn smile, even if it costs me my life."

"Can you promise to come home?"

My body stiffens at his words, knowing he's right. I'm heading into a war zone tomorrow. Nothing is guaranteed over there. "This is the last time I'm leaving, man. I'm getting out after this and coming home to find a job and putting down roots. Tyson's Creek is my home."

"That doesn't matter." Beckett slams his fist down on the table. "You can make all the plans in the world, but can you promise not to die? Promise to come back from a war zone in one piece?"

"You know I can't promise that." My shoulders sag, feeling the weight of his words resting on my shoulders.

For the first time, I feel like whatever this is between Emersyn and me is a mistake. I love her more than my own life, but can I really expect her to spend the next year alone, waiting to start our life together? The plan was always to wait until my contract was up and hope she felt the same for me, but now that she's told me how she feels, everything has changed.

"But it's not your decision to make, Beckett. It's hers. By some miracle, she has chosen to love me."

"She's going to be turning twenty-one in a few weeks, and she graduates in two years. She has her whole life ahead of her." Beckett takes a deep breath before pushing to his feet. "You are a Marine, headed off to war. You could be killed, left behind, or taken by the enemy. There are so many things that can happen to you, things out of your control. You can't promise me you'll come home to her, no matter how much both of you may want that to happen."

My mind races at the implications of what Beckett is saying. Emersyn has her whole life ahead of her. Do I want her sitting by the window every day, terrified that a man in a uniform is going to come and tell her that something has happened to me? My mind knows that Beckett is right. Bitterness courses through my veins that fate could be so cruel. That I'd be given a glimpse of the future I've longed for and have it all taken away in an instant. I have a duty to my country. We both know that, but this is the last time.

Now I remember why I've been so hesitant to tell Emersyn how I feel. It isn't that I'm afraid of losing our friendship or that I don't love her with all my heart. It's because I can't promise to come home.

"I know I can't convince you to stop loving my sister, but I ask that you give her time. Time to fall in love, to live her life, and be happy. Stay away from my sister." He begins strolling towards me. "Until you can promise to give Emersyn the life she deserves, stay away from her."

I open my mouth to respond, but he holds up his hand.

"I mean it, Brady. We've been best friends since we met in peewee football, but this is my sister. The one person I've sworn to protect with my life. Friends or not, I'll end you if you come anywhere near her before then."

I look my friend directly in the eye, seeing the conviction of his words shining back at me, and nod my head. "Okay," I respond in defeat as he places a strong hand on my shoulder and squeezes.

"You're a good man, Brady Thomas. If things between the two of you are meant to be, she will still be here when you get back. But if you are expecting to get my blessing, you're going to be waiting a long time." He gives me a sad smile before striding toward the back door and heading inside to rejoin the party.

I'd like to say that I told Beckett to fuck off, but I didn't. Instead, I left right after that, hiding away at my parents' house until Seth returned the next morning so that we could head back to base and start preparing for deployment.

My stomach growls loudly, bringing my mind back to the present, and I scoff. "I guess it's time for chow."

Slamming my laptop shut, I push back from my desk and storm out of my tent toward the mess hall. I only take a few steps before I notice Seth leaving his tent, heading for the mess hall, as well. Seth and I have been practically inseparable since they placed us in the same bunk about five years ago. On the surface, Seth and I have nothing in common. Seth's parents died when he was young—I think he said he was around eight years old. He had no other family and was placed into the foster care system, bouncing from house to house until he enlisted in the Marines a few months before his eighteenth birthday.

"Finally decided to join the land of the living?" I snicker, trying to get his attention as we approach the entrance and head inside.

The only response Seth gives me is a grunt as he grabs a tray and begins piling on food. His brown eyes are filled with sadness, and his jaw clenches tightly shut. I can practically hear his teeth grinding against themselves as he walks by. That only means one thing: Bristol didn't answer again.

When I asked Seth to attend one of Bristol's yoga classes to help her get her certification, I had no idea it would turn his entire world upside down. The minute she walked into the room, his entire personality changed. Gone was the sullen introvert whom I had to practically beg to come for a visit with me, instead replaced by a man on a mission to claim his girl. Too bad for him that Bristol was having none of that. I don't know too much about Bristol's history, but military men are apparently not her cup of tea.

It took Seth months to get Bristol to admit she wanted to be more than just his friend, and from what Seth had told me, they spent one amazing night together. Bristol wanted one night together, no strings attached, but to Seth, it was so much more. We both knew we were shipping out and didn't want to have either of our girls waiting for us to return. However, unlike me, Seth took the small piece of Bristol she was willing to give him in hopes that he'd return safely.

"So talkative today." I roll my eyes as he heads toward a table in the back. I quickly grab my own tray, fill it with some food, and follow behind him.

Seth has always been a man of few words. The opposite of me. Where I'm outgoing and love to be around people, Seth is the quiet type. He'd rather have his nose buried in a book than go out to a party. And you can forget about getting him to talk to someone he doesn't know. It took me a while, but somehow, I wore him down. I knew that Seth needed someone to care for him, to be his family, and I was more than happy to be that person for him. I chuckle softly as I remember the first time Seth came home to Tyson's Creek with me when we were on leave after deployment. The entire town was decked out in American flags, with signs welcoming their local hero home. We couldn't go anywhere in town without someone wanting to shake his hand and ask him how he was doing.

At first, he seemed beyond uncomfortable, but the more everyone accepted him, the more he discovered we were all family to each other. He began to relax and learned the names of the few people we ran into frequently around town. It took a few visits, but he started to understand that this was just how the people of Tyson's Creek were. They took care of their own, for better or worse. They were more like one enormous family instead of a town, and now he was one of us.

"Seriously, man. Who pissed in your Wheaties?" I ask, taking a seat across from me.

"Just trying to figure out what the hell I want to do when my contract is up," Seth mumbles before shoving food into his mouth.

"You could always come home with me," I respond matter-of-factly, knowing that Tyson's Creek is the perfect place for him to settle down. "My dad told me they're looking for guys at the station. Since we're in the military, all we have to do is pass the civil service exam and then attend the academy. Nothing too hard."

My parents claimed Seth as one of their own after

his first visit. He came home with me for every leave period or holiday since I met him, not that my mom would have let him get away with not coming. I swear if I showed up on my parents' doorstep without Seth in tow, my mom would walk right past me toward the car. Both my parents have been asking what his plans are after deployment, and now I may finally have an answer for them.

"Maybe." His eyes narrow slightly, no doubt thinking of how things could be between him and Bristol if he came to Tyson's Creek for good. "But don't we have to wait for a date to open for retirement?"

"Yeah, but I doubt you'd have to wait too long. Besides, maybe you could work at Ace & Hammer Construction company with me until a spot opens at the station."

Brady met Vance and Connor, the owners of Ace & Hammer, a few times during his visits to Tyson's Creek. We may be a few years older than them, but I've always been cool with those two. My mom keeps me up on all the gossip in town in her letters. She's made it a point to let me know that Vance and Connor started a construction business after I enlisted and that I have a job with them if I want it.

They both confirmed that the last time I was home, offering Seth and me a job, once we decided to retire from the Marines. Apparently, they took business classes while they worked on building their company from scratch. Since there weren't many construction businesses in the area, business came in slowly until it exploded after doing a job in Magnolia. I guess tearing down an old farmhouse to the studs and rebuilding most of it in about a week is good for business.

I doubt Seth has thought about their offer since we shipped out, but that's what I'm here for. Giving him the perfect excuse to come back to Tyson's Creek with me.

"What the hell do you know about construction?"

"Honestly, I don't know jack shit about it, but after being in the Marines for all these years, we have to do something physical. It's either that or lose our minds from boredom," I answer quickly.

Seth nods in agreement. We've been nothing more than glorified grunts since joining the Marines, doing anything and everything that is asked of us—not that we've had much of a choice. Orders are orders—so, a little manual labor isn't anything new.

"Where am I going to stay?"

"As if my parents will let you stay anywhere but with us. Besides, you can crash with me in the apartment above their garage. It's nothing fancy, but it's more space than we've had in a long while."

Seth is insane if he thinks he's going to be anywhere than with me and my parents. Hell, it took my dad and me weeks to convince my mom to let me stay in the apartment above the garage instead of renting it out again. If she had her way, Seth and I would be sleeping in bunk beds in my old room, where she could mother us to death.

"But seriously, where else are you going to go? I'm the only family you have. Besides, this will give you a chance to prove to your girl you're not going anywhere."

And maybe even help me with mine.

Seth confided in me about his feelings for Bristol, and we've been trying to come up with the perfect plan to woo her ever since, but keep coming up empty. I should've told him about Emersyn, but who knows if she'll even be around when I come home. The wounds on my heart are just starting to heal, even if only slightly; the last thing I want to do is rip them open again with the hope that things will be different.

"Bristol is not my girl," Seth mutters as he stands up, grabs his tray, and turns toward the exit. "She made it perfectly clear she wanted nothing else to do with me after that night."

I grasp Seth's shoulder, pulling him to a stop. "But you never told her everything, did you?"

He shakes his head, wrenching my arm from his grasp. "She has no idea we're coming home for good after this deployment."

"Tyson's Creek is a small town. I'm sure someone has told her that we are coming home."

"That doesn't change anything," Seth murmurs,

tossing his tray into the trash and stomping off toward his tent.

I hesitate for a minute, deciding if it's best to give him time to cool off. Who am I to give him advice about getting his girl? All it took was a few harsh words from Beckett to send me running. He was right, but I could've stayed and fought for her, for us. Instead, I turned tail and ran, and I've been running ever since.

I could've responded to any of the emails Emersyn sent me. She would detail her day, tell me what class she was taking, and all the tiny details that I was missing by being halfway across the world. I read every single one repeatedly, but never once responded. I would start typing out a response but would delete it immediately. I knew the moment I replied to her emails, I'd be taking away her chance to move on without me. I know eventually she will stop messaging me. She'll forget all about me and move on. It's what I want for her, but why does just thinking about it tear my heart in two?

Instead of letting my friend sulk, I chase after him and storm into his tent. I find him lying in his bunk, his feet crossed at the ankles as he stares up at the ceiling.

"Damn it, Seth. Stop being so stubborn!" I smack his boots hard with my hand before pushing his feet off the bed, then I plop down in their place. "I've never known you to give up so easily."

"I make decisions that could cost someone their life

almost daily. I have to be sure about them," he growls before sitting up and resting his elbows on his knees.

"Would it kill you to take a chance?"

Man, do I sound like a fucking hypocrite. Here I am, convincing Seth to take a chance at being with Bristol, and I never even tried to do the same with Emersyn. I was so worried about what she might be losing by being with me that I never thought about what we were both losing by choosing to be apart from each other.

Seth and I stare at each other in silence for a few moments before I speak. "I know how much she means to you. Ever since that party at Tranquility Retreat, you've been different. You've been looking forward to your life after the military."

"What the hell is that supposed to mean?"

"You've never thought about getting out. You've never once said anything about what you wanted to do after retirement until that night. Now you're trying to make plans for the future. Plans that could easily include Bristol if you let them."

"When did you become so fucking demanding, man?" He smirks in my direction. "Give that buddy of yours a call. I don't have any plans for after my contract is up. Might as well keep bothering your ass."

I jump up and whoop loudly. "I knew you just needed an excuse."

"No. I just want more of your mama's cooking."

"Best damn fried catfish you've ever tasted," I

preen, and my mouth waters, thinking of the fish fry my mom made us before we left.

"It's the *only* catfish I've ever tasted."

"Hence why it's the best." I slap him on the back before hurrying out of the tent to make that phone call.

I smile to myself as I grab the sat phone and plug in Vance's number. Seth is going to join me back home in Tyson's Creek. Thankfully, Seth isn't as big of an idiot as I am and has every intention of claiming his girl once we are back stateside. I have no doubt in my mind that things between Seth and Bristol will work out. Those two are meant for each other.

As for me and Emersyn... Well, I've spent most of the deployment pushing her way. At some point, she is going to move on and find someone else. Someone who can be there for her every day like she deserves. Beckett is right. There is no guarantee that I'm going to come back from this deployment. Emersyn is young and has her whole life ahead of her. I need to let her have a chance to live her life to the fullest, even if it means breaking my own heart in the process. But there's a small part of me that believes things will go back to the way they were. Once I'm home safe and sound, there will be a chance for us to be together as we always should've been.

"Let's get a move on!" I holler down the hall as I check my watch for the millionth time. "I haven't had a decent beer since we've been back."

I trudge down the hall toward the room that my friend, and former teammate Seth, is staying in.

"What the hell is taking him so long to get dressed?" I murmur.

It's been almost four months since we arrived back stateside and started our out-processing from the Marines. Since Seth didn't officially submit his retirement paperwork until halfway through our deployment, it took a little longer for him to get things settled. Now he's officially a civilian and here in Tyson's Creek for good. He had his interview with Vance and Connor this morning, even though it was nothing more than a formality, and they invited us out to have some beers to celebrate.

"I need to get my ass back into the gym," I hear Seth mumble as I stop in front of his bedroom door.

I bite my lip, attempting to hold back my laughter at the sight before me. Seth is turning back and forth, looking at his body in the mirror. Standing at a little over six feet tall, he isn't a small guy by any means, but a lot of the bulk in his muscles has disappeared. That's what happens when your plans no longer consist of more than just lifting weights and patrolling every day. Both of us have started sporting scruffy beards that cover the bottom half of our faces now that we are no longer required to shave daily.

"If you're finished checking yourself out, I'm ready to grab some beers." I cross my arms over my chest and lean against the doorframe.

"Shut the fuck up, asshole," he growls.

I enter the room, stopping beside him and looking at my reflection in the mirror. "You're still God's gift to womankind, and you know it. Almost as sexy as me."

My body hasn't changed much since returning home. My skin is still a golden brown from my days spent in the sun at the construction sites. My arms and ab muscles are just as defined as they were when I was doing PT twice a day, but my hair is no longer in a crew cut. I keep it cut short on the sides, but the top is longer, falling freely into my face at times unless I style it into that just-out-of-bed look that all the ladies love. But there's a deep pain in my eyes that I never noticed before, although I have a feeling it's been there since I walked away from Emersyn. It's like my soul is calling out to the universe, searching for its other half.

"That's why you spend your evenings playing video games and lifting weights all alone."

Seth instantly touches a nerve. People seem to think all I can do is play video games and joke around, but that's only a distraction. Something to keep my mind off the one thing I want more than anything: Emersyn. She's been the only thing I could think about since I stepped foot back in Tyson's Creek, but instead of running to her the first chance I had, I've hidden away. Choosing to stay locked away in this apartment and play video games, only leaving to head to work at Ace & Hammer.

The guys have asked me to go out for drinks a few times, but I've always declined. The only real place to hang out around here is Beckett's bar, Crawdaddy's, and that's the last place I want to go since I'm avoiding him, too. Yeah, I'm a coward. But after spending the last two years digging sand out of my underwear every day, it's good to be somewhere I don't have to sleep with one eye open. I've loved serving my country in the United States Marine Corps for the last twenty years, but now it's time to begin my life anew. Instead of being told what to wear and how to speak, I'm free to make my own decisions.

Well, almost.

"Everyone has their reasons," I snap at Seth before storming out of the room, not waiting for him to respond.

If anyone could understand how I'm feeling right now, it'd be him. He knows exactly how the desire to search for the woman you love and to beg for her forgiveness can become almost as natural as breathing. How the need to have her at your side can be so overwhelming that your soul aches with need.

I've tried to convince Seth to at least leave Bristol a message every time he calls, but he always chickens out for some reason. After a while, I stopped asking because I was doing the same thing. I never once responded to Emersyn's emails or letters to tell her what was going on. To let her know that I was okay or even to explain to her why I left so suddenly and ask her to wait for me. I just ignored her, and the longer I did, the more frantic they got. My heart shattered into pieces each time I read one of her emails, knowing that I got exactly what I wanted, but I never gave up hope that maybe she still felt something for me.

And now that I'm back in town, I want nothing more than to walk into my best friend's bar and tell him how much I love his sister. That I want to spend the rest of my life making the last couple of years up to her, but I can't. Beckett's only condition was that I come home in one piece before pursuing something with his sister and I've done that. However, I doubt he anticipated me ghosting her my entire deployment. It won't be as simple of a fix as he originally anticipated. That's not his fault, it's mine. I made my bed, and now I have to lie in it. Emersyn deserves the world, and right now, I can't give that to her. Sure, I have some money saved up and a temporary job, but nothing permanent. Nothing that will show Beckett and everyone else that I can be someone Emersyn can depend on. Someone who can take care of her. Besides, after everything I've put her through for the two last years, I doubt she would give me the time of day, let alone love me as much as I will always love her.

"Let's go. I'll drive since we both know you don't understand the meaning of taking it easy." Seth's voice brings me back to the present as he glides past me toward the front door.

I follow behind him without a word. The last thing I want to do right now is explain my feelings, not that I'd know where to begin.

I climb into the car and give Seth quick directions on how to get to Crawdaddy's, the only decent bar for fifty miles. I haven't stepped foot into Beckett's bar since a few days before the going away party he threw for me before I left for deployment almost two years ago. Aside from a few emails back and forth, we haven't spoken. Apparently, catching me kissing his baby sister did more damage to our friendship than I believed.

My phone vibrates in my pocket, bringing me back

to the present, and I check the text message. "Vance said they're already there and grabbed some tables," I tell Seth as I shove the phone back into my pocket.

As we head toward the bar, I point out a few landmarks just for something to do. Seth has been to Tyson's Creek a few times and pretty much knows his way around, but the last thing I want is for him to get lost when driving around town. Sure, he can stop and ask anyone for directions, but knowing Seth, he'd rather drive around in circles before asking someone for help.

Before long, we're pulling into the parking lot. We find a spot in front of the bar quickly, then climb out of the truck and head inside. The place looks exactly like it did the last time I was here. The bar runs along the back wall, with some barstools placed in front of it. Loud music blasts through the entire room, and I see a dance floor to the left of the door, a recent addition I didn't notice until now. I continue to scan the room before I freeze, my eyes landing on the object of my affection.

Emersyn looks more beautiful than the last time I saw her. Her lithe body sways to the music, arms raised above her head. Her usually curly hair hangs down around her shoulders, the ends brushing the skin beneath her breasts. My eyes stop as I watch her run her fingers through her hair, down her sides, tracing her hourglass figure.

"What the hell?" Seth shouts as he bumps into me.

I'm unable to break free of my trance. I ball my hand into a fist as I notice all eyes on her and her friend, Sophie. Sophie's eyes flick to mine as the pair dance together, putting the entire room under their spell. Emersyn's face is alight in glee as a man slides up behind her, wrapping his arm around her waist and pulling her closer to him. The need to rip the two of them apart and demand what the fuck is going on overcomes me. My eyes remain locked on the pair as Sophie leans over to whisper in her ear, pointing toward Seth and me standing near the edge of the dance floor.

Emersyn's eyes flick to mine as she smirks in my direction, her arms wrapping around the man's neck. She doesn't break eye contact with me as she pulls his head down to her neck, tilting her head to the side as he nuzzles his nose into her neck and grinds against her.

"You've got to be fucking kidding me," I growl as I spin on my heels and turn in the opposite direction.

I deserve this. Every minute of it after what has happened and I know it, but there's also a small part of me that wishes I could have delayed seeing Emersyn and whomever has managed to capture her heart. I didn't expect it to hurt as much as it does, but this is what I wanted. I ignored her emails and attempts to contact me since I left on deployment in hopes that she'd move on and live her life to its fullest instead of waiting here for me to return. I don't know what I was expecting when I saw Emersyn for the first time in almost two years, but this isn't it. I tried to get her to forget me, ignoring all her emails, letters, and care packages. I hoped that if I pretended she didn't exist, she'd forget me. But at the same time, I also hoped that she'd remain faithful to the small moment we shared before we left.

"Seth! Brady! Over here!" Vance calls as we get closer to the small grouping of tables.

Seth makes small talk with Vance and Connor; my eyes never stray from Emersyn on the dance floor. I watch as she continues to sway to the music, the guy's hands sliding up and down her curves as she rests her head on his shoulder, her eyes closed, and a soft smile gracing her lips. I curl my hands around the arms of the chair, anchoring myself in place. *This is what I wanted*, I remind myself. I wanted her to move on, to forget about me and live her life.

"You guys want a drink?" one of the guys asks.

I nod in response, not bothering to pay attention to who's asking, trying to maintain the rage coursing through me. I continue to glance at Emersyn on the dance floor, the desire to rip that asshole's arms off and beat him within an inch of his life surging inside me. The idea of him laying his hands on what's mine makes my blood boil and a murderous rage cloud my vision. My eyes clench shut as I fight the fury coursing through my veins. No, Emersyn is not mine. Not anymore, and it's my own fault.

But she could be, my heart whispers, willing me to go to her, to tell her that I made a mistake and that I love her deeply. That I'd spend the rest of my life making the last two years up to her if she only gave me a chance. But I can't do any of those things, not yet at least.

"Take a picture. It'll last longer," Seth jibes.

"Fuck you," I growl as I notice Beckett approaching the table.

I would love nothing more than to take my anger out on Beckett. He's my friend and was only trying to look out for his baby sister when he warned me away from her. But I can't bring myself to forgive him. Not with Emersyn here, in the arms of some asshole, gloating right in front of my face. If it wasn't for my cowardice, that could be me with my arms wrapped around Emersyn's waist, pressing against her back as I nibble along the curve of her neck and whispering how much I love and miss her in her ear. And part of the reason we aren't together is standing in front of me. If things were different, I'd greet Beckett with a smile, shake his hand, and try to get things back to normal, but right now, I can't take my eyes off Emersyn.

"Leave her alone, Brady."

My eyes snap to Beckett; his eyes narrow, daring me to continue ogling his sister.

Seth rattles off an order, but I refuse to back down. Beckett asked me to stay away from his sister until I returned, so I don't know what his issue is anymore. It also might have something to do with the fact that I completely ignored any attempt that Emersyn made to contact me while I was gone. My mind drifts to the last email she ever sent me. The way she begged me to respond, to let her know if I meant what I said before I left. Every word I read ripped a fresh hole into my heart. I could feel the pain in her words and could picture the tears streaming down her face as she told me goodbye, but I did nothing. And now I have the pleasure of watching her live her life with someone who isn't me. This is what I thought I wanted, but in reality, it's pure agony.

"Coming right up." The sound of Beckett's voice brings my mind back to the present as Seth tries to hand him his credit card. "No charge. On the house," Beckett responds as the others send up a cheer at the free drinks coming shortly.

"What was that all about?" Seth asks.

Just as I open my mouth, Emersyn strolls up to the table.

"Hey, Brady." Her honey-brown eyes sparkle with amusement as she scans the table before greeting everyone else. "Gentlemen."

I preen like a peacock at her attention. Her voice glides across my skin as I breathe in the scent of lilacs and honey, two things that will always remind me of her. My heart jumps at the thought that there may still be hope for us yet, but I remember the guy from earlier and the way she let his hands roam all over her body.

My shoulders sink as the reality of my situation sinks in. She has her whole life ahead of her. She's getting ready to graduate from college soon and start her life, probably far away from this small town near the Tennessee-Alabama border. We continue to stare at each other as something flashes behind her eyes, but it's gone in an instant.

"And what are you doing here, little lady?" Tony says from his seat next to Seth as the others whistle softly.

I growl under my breath, wanting nothing more than to rip out their throats for the impure thoughts I'm sure they are having about her. I grip the chair arms, ready to teach those men a lesson, as Seth shakes his head, warning me against the decision.

"Just came to say hello to a friend." Emersyn smiles softly at Tony, quickly winking in his direction before turning her attention back toward me.

Gone is the girl I left without a word two years ago. She's been replaced by the woman standing before me. Yes, her body has changed in the best way possible, but she even carries herself differently, commanding the attention of everyone in the room. Not just with her beauty, but her presence alone draws everyone to her, men and women alike.

My eyes catalog every detail of her body, noticing all the small changes that have occurred over the last two years as her eyes bore into my soul. Her curves are a little more pronounced, giving her a perfect hourglass figure. I lick my lips, imagining the taste of her skin as I explore each and every part of her, from the swell of her breasts to her apple bottom.

"Emersyn," I reply tersely before grabbing my beer and turning my attention toward the bar.

There are a million things I want to say to her, but my lips stay clamped tightly shut. Beckett eyes me skeptically, his eyes shifting between the two of us as he serves her friends their drinks. It's not like I have a chance at Emersyn's heart anyway. It's time to put the past behind me and move forward.

"Who's your friend?" Emersyn motions toward Seth, her hand caressing the back of his chair as she leans her hip against the table, drawing my eyes to her body once again.

She's toying with me, and I hate it—not that I don't deserve her ire or anything else she wants to throw my way. I inhale deeply, attempting to claim my anger, but say nothing. Our eyes remained locked on each other's as she waits for me to respond. Her smile falls slightly as her eyebrows pull down in confusion, her eyes scanning me as if searching for something.

"Seth," he supplies, breaking the spell she has me under. I turn my attention toward him, his eyebrow raised in question as he takes another a swig from his beer.

I don't deny my desire for her. I want—no, I *need* —her to understand how much I want her. How much I've always wanted her. I try to convey all of this with my eyes, unable to form the words to explain everything to her right here and now. That I kept my distance because I was worried about the chance I wouldn't come home. That I want to be a better man for her. I fucked up and was a coward. I should've let her know everything; I shouldn't have let her brother's words and fear keep us apart. But I don't say anything.

Her cheeks pink, and she crosses her arms over her chest, eyes dropping slightly. It seems Emersyn is just as affected by this encounter as I am. She is hiding behind her fake smile and bravado, but she can't hide from me forever. Now I can see it all, her true emotions. She wants me as much as I want her.

"Hey. I'm Emersyn." The carefree mask she had on her face when she came to the table a few minutes earlier is back in place as she breaks our gaze and focuses back on Seth.

"Nice to meet you," he continues.

"The pleasure is all mine," Emersyn purrs as she stands back to her full height, her eyes flicking towards mine as if she's afraid I'll disappear if she looks away for a single moment.

We continue having a silent conversation as I attempt to relay all my feelings to her in these few moments.

I want you.

I need you.

I'm sorry.

I love you.

Tears gather in her eyes as I lean forward, wanting to wrap her in my arms and let her know everything is okay, but one of the jackoffs at the table interrupts our conversation. I narrow my eyes slightly, daring him to say another word and risk my wrath.

"Run along, Emersyn. We have better things to do than play babysitter." I wince, knowing that, once again, I've let my anger get the best of me.

Her entire body recoils from me as if I slapped her. Hurt and confusion flash in her eyes before it's quickly replaced with pure rage. I have no right to be angry right now. Emersyn has every right to spend time with whomever she wants, even the assholes sitting across from me, but that doesn't mean I have to like it. Emersyn doesn't deserve to be treated this way. She deserves to be treated like the queen she is, but I can't stop the torrent of emotions raging through my body as the realization of our situation hits me: Emersyn has moved on, just like I wanted her to, and there's nothing I can do about it.

"Why are you such an asshole?" Her voice catches slightly as she places both hands on her hips.

"It comes naturally," I bite out, taking a sip of my beer and cocking my head toward her table. "Your friends are waiting."

Emersyn turns, finally noticing her friends waving to get her attention.

"See you around, Brady," she snipes back before turning around and sauntering back toward her group.

I watch as she steps between two of her friends, not even sparing me a second glance.

"Is there a particular reason you were such an asshole to her, and Beckett looks like he's damn near ready to take your head off?" Seth slaps me on the back of my head, but I don't pay him any mind.

My eyes are still focused on Emersyn as her twinkling laughter drifts across the bar.

"If your mama knew how you acted with that girl, she would tan your hide."

"Good thing she'll never know," I grumble, rubbing the back of my head.

After a few more moments, I tear my eyes away from Emersyn and join the conversation, finally learning the names of the three unfamiliar faces at the table.

We spend a few more hours at the bar before

heading back to our apartment. Thankfully, Seth understands my need for silence and doesn't ask me about the tension between Beckett, Emersyn, and me.

After tonight, there's one thing I am absolutely sure about. I need to come up with a plan to stay as far away from Emersyn as I can, in our small hometown, where everyone knows everyone's business.

Yeah, easier said than done.

three

emeryn

"Don't pay any attention to him," Sophie whispers into my ear as she rests her arm across my shoulders, leading me toward the bar and our other three friends.

"Easier said than done," I scoff, plopping down on the barstool between Rachel and Tasha.

I spent the last two years, and then some, worrying myself sick about Brady Thomas. Now here he is, seated at a table in my brother's bar, Crawdaddy's, without a care in the world. I poured my heart out to Brady that night, and he promised me everything would be okay. But instead of coming back inside after his showdown with my brother, he disappeared. He never came back to the party, nor answered any of the texts I sent over the next few days. And the next thing I know, he left. He didn't even have the balls to tell me he was leaving. I found out when I overheard his mom talking about it with Selina at Just the Drip.

Tears collect at the corners of my eyes as I brush my

fingers against my lips, remembering the joy I felt when he told me he felt something for me. What that something was, I have no idea. At this point, I'm starting to think I imagined everything. I emailed him and sent letters and care packages—everything I'd been doing since he joined the Marines. Instead of getting the usual responses, there was nothing. I pleaded with him to respond, worried that something horrible had happened to him, and now he's back in Tyson's Creek, acting as if none of that had happened.

"Turn that frown upside down, Em. It's my birthday!" Tasha shouts as she grabs a shot glass off the counter and throws it back.

Her brown hair is pulled into a high ponytail, the ends brushing against the collar of her shirt as she brings her head up and slams the shot glass on the bar top. Her blue eyes shine brightly as she throws her arms up in the air and whoops loudly, her hips swaying to the music. I snicker softly as her purple fitted shirt lifts slightly, showing a sliver of her belly above the jean mini skirt she borrowed to wear tonight.

"Slow down there, Tash. We have all night." Rachel giggles, her green eyes alight with mischief as she grabs her own glass and takes a shot.

Rachel slides off the stool and starts dancing with Tasha. The multicolored lights from the dance floor reflect against her black leather pants as she runs her hands through her caramel-brown hair, lifting it off her neck and pinning it to the top of her head.

Tasha and Rachel became friends with Sophie and me when we were all partnered together on a project for school a few months after Brady left for deployment. We hit it off immediately, even though Sophie was a little skeptical about them being younger than us. It didn't take long for both of them to win her over, and we've been thick as thieves ever since. Just like Sophie and me, Tasha and Rachel have been friends since childhood. We all decided instead of bar hopping near campus, we'd take the almost two-hour drive to Tyson's Creek to party for Tasha's birthday.

"We've barely had anything to drink!" Tasha says, laying her head on my shoulder and tipping her chin up.

Her eyes, glassy and slightly red, show how gone she really is. Tasha is a lightweight; it doesn't take much to get her tipsy. The problem is going to be getting her to slow down and start pacing herself, or she's going to end up hugging the porcelain goddess before the end of the night.

"You're such a cheap date." I brush a few loose strands of hair off Tasha's face, my eyes locking with Sophie over her head.

"Let's get you some water." Sophie threads her arm through Tasha's and sits her up. Once we she's sure

Tasha can sit there on her own, Sophie hops onto the bar and swings around to the other side.

If we were at any other bar in the world, Sophie wouldn't be able to just hop behind the bar and grab our friend a glass of water. But this isn't just any bar; it's my brother's, and Sophie does what Sophie wants. So instead of flagging down Beckett or another server, she grabs an empty glass and begins filling it with water.

"But I want to drink some more," Tasha whines.

Today's Tasha's twenty-first birthday. With her being the last one of us to cross the milestone, we thought it was only fitting to come to my brother's bar, but I thought we would make it a little longer than a few hours before she was plastered. Living in a small southern town, there isn't much else to do unless you enjoy tipping cows. Don't knock it. It's more fun than you think.

"And I want a million dollars." I giggle, shoving the glass of water closer to her.

"It's my birthday!" Tasha shouts, causing the entire bar to erupt in cheers around us.

"Drink some water first, and then we can talk about getting you another drink."

"You should be nicer to me. It's not our fault that the guy didn't want to give you the time of day."

"Seriously, Tasha," Rachel and Sophie hiss in her direction as my entire body stiffens.

I haven't spoken much to any of the girls about

Brady in months. Tasha and Rachel know the basics, but not the whole story. The only person who knows all the dirty details about what went down with Brady is Sophie. She held me close when I couldn't stop the tears from coming, and she sat right next to me as I obsessively watched the news, looking for any hint that something had happened to Brady.

Tears fill my eyes as Sophie throws her arm over my shoulder and pulls me into her side. "Tasha didn't mean anything by it. She's wasted," she whispers into my ear as I swipe angrily at my cheek.

"I know," I whisper as Rachel throws her arm over my shoulder.

"No one said falling in love was easy. If it was, everyone would do it." Rachel plants a messy kiss on my cheek as Beckett places a shot glass full of pink liquid in front of me.

"What is it?" I question.

"It's delicious. Just drink it, and stop pining after someone who isn't good enough for you," he grumbles as he grabs our empty glasses and drops them into the bin below the bar.

I roll my eyes, not wanting to have this conversation with him again. I laid into Beckett after Brady left, and he told me about warning Brady off. At first, I was furious at him for sticking his nose into my business, but as the months passed with no word from Brady, I started to understand. I didn't put my life on hold, by any means. I went to class and hung out with my friends, but every time I came home, I went searching for information about Brady. I was plastered to the television, listening to anything and everything I could about what was going on in the region where I assumed Brady's unit was located.

If only I'd known that was the last time I'd see Brady for almost two years. If I'd realized that could have been the last time I'd feel his arms around me or the caress of his lips against my skin, I'd have done everything differently. I never would have left him alone to face my brother's wrath. I'd have stood proudly next to him, letting anyone who would listen know that he belonged to me. I would've told Beckett to mind his business and that I wasn't a little girl anymore. That no matter how hard he fought it, there was nothing he could to do stop me from loving Brady. But hindsight is always twenty-twenty.

"You never think anyone is good enough for me, big brother," I clip out before throwing back the shot. "*That asshole* is your best friend."

"Best friend or not, I won't let him hurt my baby sister."

The fruity liquid travels down my throat, burning slightly on its way down. Beckett and Brady may be best friends, but I'll always be his only baby sister. Beckett was always there to hold me when I cried or would send Brady an email when the stress of not knowing how he was doing became too much for me. He was so worried about what the fear and stress of not knowing if Brady was coming home or not would do to me, but even without the two of us being together, it still happened anyway. I love Brady. I'd worry about him, whether he was overseas protecting our country or living down the road. It's the same reason our mom makes us text her when we are leaving and arriving somewhere. It used to annoy me when I was younger, but now I understand. It isn't because she doesn't think we are capable of taking care of ourselves or that she wants to keep tabs on our whereabouts at all times; it's because she loves us. That is the part of all this Beckett is missing, but there is nothing I can say to make him understand. He believes he is responsible for all the hurt and pain I feel because he is the one who kept Brady and me apart, but it isn't his fault. He has tried every day since Brady left our house before deployment to ease the pain. And now, I have no doubt he'll do anything to protect me from Brady breaking my heart a second time.

"When are you going to realize that we're all grown up now, Beckett?" Sophie chimes in.

She winks at my brother before lifting her shot glass to her lips and sipping it. "Delicious," she purrs as she runs her tongue along the rim of the glass.

Beckett's eyes focus on the path of her tongue, growing wider as she continues licking her way around the glass. The rest of us stifle our giggles. The three of us have watched Sophie try to get Beckett to notice her for close to a year, but with every step forward she makes, she takes another two backward.

My brother's entire demeanor changes before my eyes. He's no longer the overprotective brother, but a man who has met his match. His eyes darken as the two of them stare at each other, daring the other to look away. Sophie raises her eyebrow at him before crossing her arms under her breasts, lifting them slightly.

Beckett's cheeks flush as he turns away, attempting to focus on everything but Sophie.

"When you start acting like one," he growls before spinning on his heels and heading toward the other end of the bar to check on a customer.

Sophie's shoulders sink as she watches his retreating form. "One of these days, he's going to give in to me."

"Everyone with a pair of eyes can see how much he wants you." I give Sophie a smile before grasping her hand and giving it a squeeze. "But my brother is a tough nut to crack."

I have a feeling that wanting to be with Sophie isn't Beckett's problem at all; it's his feeling of inadequacy. Beckett has never left Tyson's Creek for more than a few weeks for vacation. He worked at Crawdaddy's all through high school, and when the Crawfords decided they wanted to relocate to Florida to be closer to their children, he decided to buy the place. He's been running it ever since.

Most people would say that means Beckett has a good head on his shoulders, but to Beckett, it just means he's had a bout of good luck. According to him, I and, by default, Sophie, have the world at our fingertips. We should travel, see the world, and follow all our dreams after graduation. Leave Tyson's Creek in our rearview mirror. But what he has never understood is that neither of us wants to move to the big city, or even leave Tyson's Creek. Sophie wants to be wherever I am, and everything I've ever wanted is right here.

"I wish they'd just fuck and get it over with—put all of us out of our misery," Tasha says loudly, and we all burst out laughing.

"Leave it to the drunk one to state the obvious." Sophie bumps her shoulder, and Tasha stumbles slightly, almost tumbling to the floor. "*Whoa*, there, drunkie! The last thing we need is to get kicked out of the only bar in town."

"As if Beckett would let his precious baby sister drink anywhere else." Rachel rolls her eyes as she waves at Beckett, trying to get his attention. "Besides, we can drink here for free, as long as our girl Em is here with us."

Rachel throws her arms over my shoulder, but I push it off. "Is that why you're friends with me?"

Her eyes widen, and I smile, letting her know I'm only kidding.

"What can I get you ladies?" Beckett asks.

"Four Stellas, please," Sophie purrs, resting her elbows on the bar and leaning forward slightly, giving Beckett a perfect view down her shirt.

Beckett's eyes remain locked on Sophie's. "The only way a man will respect you is if you respect yourself."

"Why are you so dense?"

Beckett's eyes immediately narrow as he curls his hand into a fist by his side.

"We're waiting." Sophie motions toward the end of the bar.

He always keeps bottles of cider and light beer for the four of us, knowing we won't drink any of the IPAs or dark beers his regulars favor. It pays to be the bartender's baby sister.

Without a word, he turns and heads down to the other end of the bar, grabbing the four beers, handing them to one of the servers, and pointing in our direction. She saunters over, places them in front of us, and says hello.

"Why do you always have to push his buttons?" I turn toward Sophie, peeking at Brady and his friends sitting at the table a few feet away.

"I'm not pushing his buttons," she responds innocently, but I raise my eyebrow at her. "Okay, well, not on purpose."

"Fair enough." I giggle, taking a healthy pull from my beer.

"Remind me why we come here?" Sophie spins around in her chair, crossing her long legs across each other.

"For the fine pieces of man meat we get to look at." Rachel nods toward the group as she spins around on her stool, her eyes focusing on one of the new guys in town.

"Vance and Connor are taken," I deadpan, not wanting my friends to be on the receiving end of their wives' wrath.

Audrey and my boss, Selina, are two of the sweetest ladies in the world...until you mess with their men. That's when the claws come out.

Audrey and her daughter, Love, moved to town a few months after Brady left on deployment, to help Bristol out at her yoga studio, Nurture Space. Business had picked up a lot around that time, and she needed help. Well, that and she was pregnant with her beautiful baby girl, Rebekah. As far as I know, the father isn't in the picture, and Bristol remains tightlipped about who he may be.

Selina and Vance were high school sweethearts, but she left town right after graduation to pursue her dream of becoming a prima ballerina. According to Becks, she escaped the confines of small-town living only to come back and buy the only dance studio in town from Ms. Cassandra. I started working at Barre Studio shortly after she purchased it, wanting to do something to keep my mind off how much I missed Brady. I had been taking classes there since I was a little girl, and although I had originally planned to major in dance, I fell in love with graphic design instead. I still take some classes and help Selina teach some when she needs me, but dancing is more of a hobby than anything else now.

"The one sitting next to Brady is Seth," I continue. "I don't know anything about the other four."

Sophie winks at me and motions toward the table of men as they push back from the table and head for the door.

"Brady is looking at you," Tasha says loudly.

Sophie clasps her hands over her mouth, and my cheeks heat with embarrassment.

"Shut up, Tash. The last thing I want is for him to think I've been watching him all night."

"You haven't?" Tasha cocks her head to the side as she tries to figure out what she missed.

The rest of us burst out laughing at her drunken ignorance.

"I have, but he doesn't need to know that," I say with a smile as I glance at the exit, locking eyes with Brady once again before he quickly turns and heads out the door.

"Don't worry, Em," Sophie murmurs. "We both know how much he wants you. He just has to admit it to himself. Besides, you need to make him work for it."

"Work for it, huh?" I scoff, shaking my head as she throws her arm over my shoulder.

"Yes. Major groveling is in order," Rachel responds, downing the last of her beer before placing the empty bottle on the bar top.

"I don't even know how he feels about me. It's been two years of waiting for him to come home and tell me how he feels about me."

"They're just words, Emersyn. He was going away to fight a war. Not to mention, your brother, who also happens to be his best friend, walked in on you moments before you could profess your undying love for each other."

"He didn't once write me, respond to my emails, or even give me any hint that he wanted to be with me."

"Brady was a little busy, don'tcha think? I don't know much, but that takes a lot of concentration." Tasha wraps her arm around other my shoulder, pulling me into a hug.

"I know," I murmur.

I know in my heart that no matter what his reasons were for not communicating with me, Brady is the one I want to spend the rest of my life with. I've loved him for most of my life, and one taste two years ago isn't enough.

four

brady

Seeing Emersyn and Beckett at Crawdaddy's last night didn't go as I expected. Not that I had any idea what to expect for our first meeting since I've been back in town.

Beckett and I have been friends since elementary school. The idea that he could never forgive me for falling in love with his kid sister is almost unfathomable. Bros before hoes, or however the saying goes. But I guess thinking of his sister as a hoe in the first place is where I went wrong.

Although Beckett is one of the main reasons Emersyn and I didn't get together before I left for deployment, I'm the reason we can't be together now. However, my anger towards Beckett for interfering in the first place gets stronger the longer I fight to keep my distance from her. My mind keeps playing the what-if game, wondering if things had worked out differently that night, would Emersyn and I be together right now?

"What the hell am I going to do?" I murmur into my empty room as I take a seat on my bed, placing my elbows on my knees.

I've spent most of the day wracking my brain for ways to repair my friendship with Beckett and have a relationship with Emersyn, but I keep coming up with nothing. He's doing his job as a big brother, protecting Emersyn from the heartache I caused with my silence. I can even understand his original reservations about me heading off to war without the promise of return, but now I'm back home safe and sound. It's time to make plans for the future. Plans that, whether he likes it or not, involve his sister. I just need to figure out how to go about it.

I doubt walking up to Emersyn the next time I see her and telling her that I plan to cherish and love her until my dying day is the best way to go about it. She doesn't have any reason to have faith in the things I say. I told her that I'd been waiting for her for so long that I didn't dare to hope that she felt something for me before I left, but then nothing. I need to find a way to prove to her that all those feelings are still there and try to find a way to explain to her why I did the things that I did. I know she won't forgive me right away—I'd be a fool to expect that—but I have to try.

Although falling in love with her wasn't intentional, it felt natural. Every man doesn't set out to ravage his best friend's baby sister or to fall in love with a woman who's over fifteen years younger than him. There are so many words I would use to describe Emersyn, but naïve isn't one of them. She has always been wise beyond her years, understanding the world around her in ways that people twice her age are incapable of.

I've watched Emersyn grow up, becoming a woman that I couldn't imagine not calling my own. Yes, she's beautiful, but it's more than just a physical attraction. I fell in love with her smile, how the room lit up the moment she entered, and her words. She always had the right words or phrases to help me through whatever I was going through.

"What's got your panties in a twist?" Emersyn takes a seat beside me, crossing her legs in front of her.

"Nothing, really," I respond, knowing she won't let that answer slide.

Emersyn has always been there for me, helping me wrap my head around hard decisions.

I've been wracking my brain all night, trying to find the right way to tell her I'm leaving, and not for some training exercise. It's time for my unit to join the fight. To protect the country from those who wish to destroy us. It's an honor to protect the ones I love, but my heart breaks at the idea of not coming home to Emersyn when it's all over.

"You know better than that." She threads her arm through mine before resting her head on my shoulder.

"I'm leaving." I sigh as I pull my arm from her grasp

and turn toward her. "My unit is shipping out next week."

Emersyn's eyes fill with tears. "How long are you going to be gone this time?"

"A year, possibly more." I grasp both her hands in mine. "I need to tell you."

"There you two are." My mom smiles down at the two of us as she steps out the back door. "It's time for dinner."

"Give us a few more minutes," I say with a forced smile, knowing I'm about to ruin everyone's appetite with my news.

"You haven't told any of them yet?" Emersyn swipes at her eyes.

"No. I wanted to tell you first."

I stand before reaching my hand out toward her. She grips it, and I pull her to her feet.

"You're my favorite girl, after all."

Emersyn smiles brightly at me. "I'm sure you say that to all the girls."

I open my mouth to respond but bite my tongue. Now isn't the time to tell her how I feel.

"No, just you. Only you." I smile at her, tucking a piece of hair behind her ear before pulling her through the back door behind me.

Something about this deployment was different. It could've been because it was my last, but the need to tell Emersyn how I felt continued to bubble inside me until I couldn't hold it in any longer.

When I saw her running out of my going away party with tears in her eyes, I knew that was my moment. I was prepared for her to let me down easily, stating all the reasons that had been holding me back. But she told me she loved me, and my heart soared. I didn't care about my friendship with Beckett or what people would say about us. All I cared about was the woman I loved more than life itself returning my feelings.

"Brady!" Seth shouts as he comes barreling through the door.

I don't know what I thought life after the military would be like, but here I am, staying in an apartment above my parents' garage with Seth and working for a friend's construction company. It's not much, but things could be so much worse.

"What set your ass on fire?" I grumble, strolling out of my bedroom and heading into the living room.

Seth's eyes shine brightly as a wide smile spreads across his face. Obviously, something good happened on his trip into town to get coffee, although I don't see any coffee in his hands.

"You need to get out. Now. Better yet, stay gone until tomorrow, just in case," he barks over his shoulder before heading into the kitchen and throwing the fridge open.

I love Seth like a brother, but he's out of his damn mind if he believes he can just kick me out of our apartment without a good reason. I follow him into the kitchen, leaning against the counter near the fridge, and wait patiently for him to finish. When he mumbles about ingredients, I clear my throat, hoping to get his attention.

After a few moments and nothing from Seth, I drop my hand in front of his face and snap my fingers, hoping to get his attention. "Earth to Seth. Care to explain to me why I need to leave my house?"

"Bristol," he grunts without even a glance in my direction.

"Holy shit," I gasp, standing up to my full height.

Only Seth could run into Bristol with minimal effort. She gave him her number before we left. Any normal person would have used it by now, but Seth had other ideas.

"Anything you need from me? Other than getting lost for the night?"

"No, nothing that I can think of. I'm gonna head to the store and figure out what I can cook for her."

Seth grabs two beers from the fridge and offers me one, probably to calm his nerves. He's talked about nothing but Bristol since we left on deployment, trying desperately to get her to speak to him, tell him to fuck off, anything.

"Sounds like a plan. You could always ask Mama

for help." I grab the beer from his hand and crack it open, taking a healthy gulp.

"I want to cook for Bristol myself."

"You've got this, man. I should hop into the shower and find something to do since you're kicking me out." I tap my beer bottle against his before pushing off the counter.

Seth has given me the perfect opportunity to talk to Beckett and find out where he stands on Emersyn and me being together. It may be a long shot, but Beckett is the perfect person to clue me in about whether I have a chance with her after everything I've put her through. Now that his reservation about me coming home is void, maybe he'll start warming up to the idea of Emersyn and me being together.

"You should call Emersyn and apologize for being a jerk last night."

"Just leave it alone, man. Emersyn is a big girl. She's just fine. I don't need to run over there and apologize for being myself." I try to leave the kitchen, but he steps in my path.

Fuck. That's exactly what I should be doing right now. I should be on my hands and knees in front of Emersyn, begging her to let me be a part of her life. But that wouldn't do me any good. I can apologize to Emersyn as much as I want, but I need to find a way to prove the depth of my feelings to her. Besides, I don't want to get into this with Seth. He has his date with

Bristol to focus on. The last thing he needs is my issues bringing him down. Seth has been waiting for two years to figure out whatever is going on between him and Bristol. The last thing he needs is my issues piled on top. Besides, I have a lot of apologizing to do before I can even think about Emersyn and me being together.

"What's going on, man?" Seth takes a pull from his beer before placing it on the kitchen table to his left. "We both know you weren't being yourself last night at all."

"Nothing." I try to push past him, but he grabs my arm.

"That doesn't sound like nothing, Brady."

"It's complicated, and to be honest, I don't even know what's going on myself."

How do I explain to Seth that I'm in love with Emersyn, but I'm not man enough to know how to tell her or even how to apologize for the two years of radio silence? Not to mention I need to figure out how to patch things up between Beckett and me. I know we will never be as close as we were before I left, but I know my best friend is still in there somewhere. I just need to figure out how to get him back on my side. That's the definition of complicated. I should have manned up two years ago and told Beckett to fuck off, but I didn't, and now I have to hope everything will work out for the best. Seth is on the verge of getting everything he hoped for. I doubt he could understand the position I'm in.

"I'm here if you need someone to talk to, all right?" Seth says before releasing my arm.

"Thanks." I give him a tight smile before continuing out of the kitchen. "I'll be out of your hair in thirty minutes."

I don't waste any time getting showered and dressed. I want to get out of the apartment as quickly as possible to ensure Seth has all the time he needs to make tonight perfect with Bristol. I pull on a pair of faded jeans and a long-sleeved gray Henley before heading out of my bedroom. I notice Seth sitting at the table, scribbling on a piece of paper.

"I'm headed out. I'll crash on someone's couch, so you don't need to worry about me showing up before morning."

He doesn't even glance in my direction as I head past him and out the front door. It would be a waste of time to talk to him now. Once he sets his mind to something, he's lost to the world.

As I make my way down the stairs, an idea comes to mind as I stride toward my parents' front door.

"Mama!" I call through the house before shutting the door behind me.

"In the kitchen," she responds.

I turn the corner and head inside.

"What brings you down? It's not dinnertime yet."

My mom smiles as she reaches down to pull something out of the oven.

Standing at just over five feet, she's the epitome of the southern woman. Salt-and-pepper dark brown hair, bright eyes that seem to know exactly what someone needs just by looking at them, and mean cooking skills. Her fish fry is the best around, and I'm not just saying that because she's my mother.

Being bachelors fresh out of the Marines, Seth and I rarely cook a meal, even though we have a full kitchen in the apartment upstairs. Why would we cook when we have the best chef in town living downstairs? As if she would let us cook, anyway. She had the entire upstairs fridge packed to the gills with food, ready and waiting for me when I came home. Cooking is the way my mom relieves stress, and she had more than enough stress worrying about Seth and me being on the other side of the world.

"Seth has a date." I reach into the bowl of freshly baked muffins sitting on the counter.

She quickly slaps my hand, using her catlike reflexes. Even at sixty-eight years old, she catches me every time. They say you're supposed to slow down with age, but in my mom's case, she's only getting faster.

"With whom?" She places her hot pie on the cooling rack, daring me to touch it.

"Bristol," I say with a smile before snatching the

muffin and rushing over to the other side of the kitchen and out of her reach.

Although my mom is missing some details about what happened with Seth and Bristol, she hasn't been living under a rock. Anyone with eyes can see those two belong together. Something flashes in her eyes, but it's gone just as quickly. It seems my mom might not be as clueless as I thought.

"What do you know, Mama?" I question as I pop the muffin into my mouth.

"Brady Michael Thomas. You're lucky I love you, boy, or I'd tan your hide!" she scolds as she grabs the bowl of muffins and places them behind her for protection.

"You'd have to catch me first," I mumble around the food in my mouth.

"Stop talking with your mouth full. Did you forget your manners while you were over there?"

"No, ma'am." I snort as I raise my eyebrow. "Are you going to answer my question?"

"No. Are you going to make nice with Beckett?" As always, my mother gets right to the heart of a situation.

"Yes, Mama. I was on my way to his house right now. We have some things to discuss."

"Like how you're desperately in love with his baby sister?"

I cough loudly, choking on the last bit of muffin in my mouth, and she smiles, thrusting a glass of water in my direction. I grab the glass and gulp half of it down. "You knew?"

I wasn't trying to hide my feelings for Emersyn from anyone, but I had hoped I wasn't walking around with my heart on my sleeve. I guess I was wrong.

"Everyone does, son. Well, except Emersyn." She grabs the glass from me and sets it in the sink. "You need to make things right with both Beckett and Emersyn. That little girl has been through so much because of you boys."

"She isn't a little girl anymore." I sigh, thinking about everything I must have put her through in the last year. "I have a lot of explaining to do."

"Yes, you do, but not to me." She places her hand on top of mine, giving it a squeeze. "Be honest with her about how you feel. Honesty is always the best policy, Brady."

I love how easy my mom believes my conversation with Emersyn should be. Emersyn has a good heart, unable to hold a grudge against anyone, but Beckett is the exact opposite.

"Thanks, Mama." I lean over and give her a quick kiss on the cheek before reaching over her shoulder and grabbing another muffin from the basket.

She shakes her head and smiles. "Now shoo before I have to make more muffins for the bake sale tomorrow and won't have enough time to finish this pie for Seth."

I wink at her as I head out the door. I knew my

mom would help Seth out with his date with Bristol, making things a little less stressful for him. I may not be able to make the conversation he's going to have with her go easier, but I can help make sure dinner goes off without a hitch.

I just wish my conversation with Beckett could be made easier with some pie from my mama.

five

emersyn

I sneak my way out of Sophie's bedroom, and the sounds of Tasha and Rachel snoring disappear the moment I pull the door shut behind me. I tip-toe toward the kitchen, not wanting to jostle my head for fear of the shooting pain I felt in my head the moment I sat up this morning.

After Brady and his friends left, the girls and I drank our weight in those delicious pink shots my brother was making for us before he piled us into the back of his truck and drove us home. I could've done without the lecture about the dangers of drinking from him, but my friends and I were all thankful for the ride home. We would've been waiting a lifetime for a taxi to show up to take our drunk asses back to Sophie's place.

I would love to say that I passed right out when I climbed into the bed with Sophie, but no such luck. Instead, I spent most of the night tossing and turning, images of Brady's face filtering through my mind. I'm not sure how I thought our reunion was going to go, but last night wasn't it. I figured he'd apologize for ghosting me and then make some excuse about being too busy or needing to focus, but the open pain and hostility coming off him in waves gave me whiplash.

Brady left me without a word for over a year. I never asked him to promise me forever, but I at least expected him to give me an answer. I laid my heart out to him that night, and I felt like he might feel the same way about me. But the moment Beckett walked out the door, everything changed. I was crushed when he didn't come back to the party, and I kept telling myself it was because he was disgusted with me, but after last night, I have a feeling that wasn't the case.

"Penny for your thoughts?" The sound of Sophie's voice right behind me causes me to jump in surprise.

"Stop sneaking up on me like that!"

"I've been standing here for almost five minutes. If you weren't so deep in thought, maybe you'd have noticed." Sophie brushes past me, heading right for the Keurig on the kitchen counter and popping in a pod. "Grab some cups. I'll make us some coffee, and then you can tell me all about it."

"There's nothing to talk about," I grumble, heading into the kitchen and grabbing two white coffee mugs from the rack before placing them on the counter beside her. "Where's your dad?"

Sophie's dad has been raising her on his own since

her mom disappeared when she was about six months old. The story goes like most others in a small town: Boy gets girl pregnant, and they get married. They think the grass is greener in the big city and decided to move and start their family somewhere else. And in this case, they went a little further away while looking for a big city, moving all the way to Atlanta. Sophie's parents planned to live happily ever after, but Sophie's mom had other plans. She handed Sophie off to a neighbor while Mr. King was at work and took off and never looked back.

Sophie's dad immediately took some time off work and moved home to be closer to his family. He didn't have any siblings, and his parents helped him out when they could, but they both passed away before Sophie and I made it to high school. No matter what, Mr. King made sure Sophie never wanted for anything when she was growing up. And, since his parents passed, my family was always there for her when she needed anything.

While we were growing up, Mr. King worked at Tranquility Retreat as a farmhand and general handyman, doing anything and everything Mr. Armstrong needed. But when Sophie and I started high school, he wanted to start saving money for her to go to college, and farming didn't pay as well as he believed. Sophie never once asked for anything, but he insisted, choosing to start driving trucks around the country to ensure his little girl continued to have everything she desired. He still drives trucks, but that also means he's not home very often. He makes sure never to miss holidays or special events, but everything else is dependent on his schedule.

"Working, of course." Sophie sighs, grabbing one of the mugs and pressing the button to start the machine. "But stop changing the subject. What's on your mind, Em?"

"Nothing special. I was trying to figure out if I had anything planned for today."

"Tell that to someone who doesn't know you." She scoffs, rolling her eyes at me for good measure.

The machine whirls to life, and the smell of hazelnut coffee begins filling the air. We stand there in silence, watching the brown liquid fill the mug before Sophie switches cups and starts the process all over again.

"You know I have unlimited patience," Sophie begins, pushing one of the glasses towards me. "You're not leaving this apartment until you tell me."

Her eyes lock with mine over the rim of the cup as she takes a healthy sip.

"I don't know how you drink coffee black." I make a disgusted noise in my throat before striding toward the refrigerator and grabbing the creamer her dad keeps in there just for me.

"I like to taste my coffee, not sugary sweet creamer."

"Don't knock it till you try it," Rachel says, and she grabs the creamer from my hand and pours a healthy amount into the unclaimed mug resting on the counter.

"That was mine, you know."

"You snooze you lose." She winks at me before taking a sip and moaning softly. "That's the good stuff."

I shake my head in her direction before grabbing two more cups from the rack and heading back over to the machine. I might as well make one for Tasha because I have a feeling she's going to be up soon, as well. Just as the second cup of coffee finishes brewing, Tasha stumbles out of the room.

"Coffee. Stat," she grumbles as I place the cup in her hands and take a seat on the sofa near Sophie.

We all sit in silence, drinking our coffee slowly while trying to wake up our sleep-addled and more than likely hung-over brains, when Sophie huffs loudly. "Okay, Em. Spill."

"Spill what?" Tasha exclaims before groaning loudly and gripping her head. "Whatever it is, do it quietly, please."

"If I know our girl, she spent the morning mooning over Brady and now is pissed at herself," Rachel responds, placing her mug on the coffee table in front of her and tucking her feet under her butt.

"Yup, that sounds like her," Sophie responds, turning her body in my direction.

"Can you stop talking about me like I'm not here?" I throw my hands in the air, but know my friends aren't going to let this go until I give them an explanation. "You're partially right. I seriously can't get the tortured look he had on his face most of the night out of my head. I just don't get it."

"Like I told you last night, Emersyn, he still cares about you. Everyone can see that, but he doesn't feel like he has a chance with you anymore."

She used my full name, so I know she means business. "What do you mean?"

"It means you didn't give him any inclination that you were still waiting for him to give you an answer. I'm not saying you should've waited by the phone for him to call, but the emails were too much."

"Emails?" Tasha and Rachel respond in unison, giving me a questioning look.

"But that was all a lie." I wince in pain but continue to stand my ground.

Those emails weren't the best decision on my part. When Brady first left, I was determined to prove to him I didn't mind waiting for him. But as the months went by without so much as a response, I decided to be petty. I know. Not one of my finer moments. It was childish and downright spiteful, but I was desperate. I just wanted him to talk to me, even if it was him telling me to fuck off.

After months of not hearing from him, I was desperate for any response from him, even a negative one. The only thing left was to try and make him respond to me. One night about a month ago, I got completely hammered at a frat party on campus. Don't worry. My girls made sure I got home safely and tucked me into bed. But the moment the door closed behind them, I hopped out of bed and headed directly for my laptop.

I wrote to him all about the guys hitting on me almost daily, the ones that followed me around campus, begging for me to give them the time a day. I told him about the guys at parties that would smile in my direction and slide up beside me, wrapping a possessive hand around my waist. And then I told him about Brian, the only guy that I even contemplated trying to be with.

"We all know this..." I murmur, my eyes looking everywhere but at my three best friends.

"We don't..." Tash responds as Rachel nods her head.

"Basically, I sent Brady an email about a month ago, telling him about all the fictitious dates I was going on and that I have a boyfriend."

"Dates and a boyfriend?" Tasha questions. "Wait, I need a second to wrap my head around this."

"Present tense?" Rachel lifts an eyebrow in question.

I nod my head, dropping my head into my hands as I groan. "I know it was childish, but I just wanted him to say something. Respond in some way to let me know he cared about whether I was alive or dead."

What I didn't include was the way I wanted to shower after each time someone who wasn't him touched me. That I measure each of those boys up to the lifetime of memories I have with him, and none of them even come close to him in my heart. I also didn't tell him that although I found Brian crazy attractive, we'd never date because he is not into members of the opposite sex.

I'd like to say it was the alcohol talking in that email, but that'd be a lie. I was desperate for some word from Brady. A hint that he was okay. A part of me assumed that jealousy was as good of an emotion as any, so why not go with that, but he still didn't respond. After a few days of constantly checking my email, I finally broke down and begged Beckett to send him an email. Beckett told me once in passing that he and Brady exchanged the occasional email, but nothing serious. Beckett never told me what was in those emails, and I never asked, but this time I had to know. At first, he didn't want to send anything, but after some convincing, he finally emailed him and heard back almost immediately. It was then I realized that Brady didn't care about me or what I had to say, but then why did he react that way in the bar last night?

"Oh, Emmie," Tash coos before pushing to her feet and wrapping me in her arms.

I hug her body tightly to mine and bury my nose in her shoulder. I can feel my other two friends wrapping their arms around us, as well. The tears I've been fighting to hold back start rolling down my cheeks as I try to figure out what to do next. I still love Brady, and at this point, I don't know if I'm capable of stopping. Even after a year apart, just seeing him for a few moments turned my entire world upside down. And after last night, I don't know what's real and what isn't anymore.

Slowly, we unwrap our arms from each other, and someone grabs my hand, spinning me around to look at them. Sophie has a soft smile on her face as she places her hands on both my shoulders. "What now?"

"What the heck do you mean, *what now*?" I sniff, swiping at my cheeks.

"What are you going to do now?" Tasha throws her arm over my shoulder. "Are you going to tell Brady the truth, or are you going to remain miserable and wonder about what could've been between the two of you?"

"I don't know," I murmur, dropping my head onto her shoulder.

"Well, I guess you have a lot to think about before leaving here today because I can guarantee you're going to run into Brady sooner rather than later," Rachel chirps, causing all of us to giggle.

Rachel is right. Tyson's Creek is a small town, not to mention Brady is my brother's best friend. Sure, they are on the outs because of me, but I know Beckett was just as worried about Brady as I was. Things between those two will go back to normal in no time. I just hope I have an answer before then.

six
brady

I took my time heading over to Beckett's place. What should have only taken me a few minutes to drive to his tiny apartment near the creek a few blocks away from Crawdaddy's took me almost an hour. What do you say to your estranged best friend after ghosting his baby sister after he catches you kissing right before you leave on deployment for Lord knows how long? Why don't they make apology cards for something like that? It would make everything so much easier to explain.

"Stop being a chickenshit and talk to him. What's the worst that could happen?" I mumble to myself as I pull into a spot in front of his apartment.

Right now, I have two choices. I can pull out of this parking spot and sleep in my truck tonight, or I can man up and go talk to the only person who can help me figure out how to get into his baby sister's good graces.

I know I owe Emersyn an explanation, if not more

than that. I doubt *sorry* is going to cover it. I hurt her by leaving town without a word after our kiss, and then on top of that, I've ignored all her attempts to contact me before we ran into each other at Crawdaddy's last night. I'm going to have to come up with something better than an apology. Nothing short of getting down on my knees and begging for her forgiveness will work. Even though there might not be anything left between us, I have to try to get her to open up to me again.

After the way she looked at me last night, seeing the longing in her eyes, I don't think I'll be able to leave her alone. There's still something there between the two of us. It might not be as intense as it was previously, but I know deep down she still has feelings for me. I just need to remind her of how she felt before I left for deployment and remind her that we can get back there again. I just need her to give me a chance to make things right between us and show her how good we could be for each other. It's going to take some major groveling on my part, and I'm going to need help. Help in the form of my best friend and her older brother, Beckett.

Beckett is Emersyn's biggest protector and one of two people standing in the way of any chance of us being together. Although we emailed back and forth a few times while I was deployed, it was always superficial. He would ask me how I was doing and if I needed anything, but no news about Emersyn. I desperately wanted to ask him if the things she was writing in her emails were true, but I knew I didn't have a right to know, especially after the last few emails she sent me.

Having made up my mind, I climb out of my truck and make my way to Beckett's apartment building, taking a deep breath before I knock on the door. I stand there for a few minutes, but when I get no response, I bang on the door a little louder this time. I don't have to wait too long before the door flies open, and a very disheveled Beckett appears before me.

My eyes widen in surprise as I take in his wild look. Beckett's usually perfectly tousled dark hair is pointing in every direction. He's shirtless, with a pair of dark green plaid pajama pants hanging loosely on his hips, making it more than obvious that I just woke him up. Fuck.

"Sorry, man." I reach up, rubbing the back of my neck in embarrassment. "I didn't even think to check the time before coming over."

He grunts in response, his hazel eyes crusted in sleep as they lock with mine. We stand there, staring at each other for a few minutes in awkward silence. I open and close my mouth a few times, trying to find the perfect thing to say, but can't think of a single damn thing. At this point, I'm just thankful that Beckett hasn't punched me yet. Lord knows I deserve it after the way I've treated Emersyn for the last two years and some change.

"Are you going to invite me in?"

"That depends." He yawns loudly, running his hand through his hair before crossing his arms over his bare chest.

"Fair." My mind continues to race, trying to think of what I can say to my estranged best friend to convince him to at least let me through the door. "I'm an asshole who's in love with Emersyn."

He doesn't say a word. Only nods his head before turning on his heels and heading back into his apartment. I follow him inside, my head swinging left to right as I take in his one-bedroom apartment.

This place hasn't changed one bit. There are a few generic pieces of art hanging on the walls around the room, giving it a lived-in feel, and I notice the same secondhand, worn L-shaped leather couch tucked into the living room to my right, facing a large flat-screen television hanging on the wall. Below the television is a dark-colored wood entertainment center with every video game console known to man tucked neatly into every available space.

"It's good to see some things never change." I chuckle as Beckett walks wordlessly into the clean open-concept kitchen, opening a few cabinets before he finds whatever he's looking for.

"I remember helping you haul this thing up the stairs the day you moved in." I run my hands along the back of the couch as I enter the living room and take a seat. "It took you, me, Riggs, and Walker almost an hour to get it up the two flights of stairs."

"Walker was ready to grab a chainsaw and cut it into pieces before we finally figured it out," Beckett responds, his voice thick with sleep. "Coffee?"

"Sure, I'll take a cup."

Beckett makes quick work of turning on the coffee pot, the smell of coffee filling the air. "So, you're still in love with my sister?"

"Yes," I respond without hesitation.

I know this is probably something I should be telling Emersyn first, but I need to ensure he knows what she means to me. That no matter what I must do or how long I have to wait for her to come back to me, I'll convince her that we belong together. But not only do I need her to know, I need Beckett to understand how much she means to me, as well. I let our friendship and his reservations about the two of us being together get in the way of our relationship before.

"Could've fooled me," he scoffs as a soft beep fills the space between us, signaling the coffee has finished. "You don't ghost someone you love for two years without a word."

Beckett has always been a straight shooter, never beating around the bush. He's been this way our entire friendship, but hearing those words out of his mouth stings.

"And whose fault is that?" I growl, cutting right to

the heart of the situation. "I'm not going to apologize for the way I feel about your sister."

"You shouldn't have been looking at her period. She's my baby sister and off limits." There's an edge to Beckett's voice that wasn't there before as he places a cup of coffee on the coffee table in front of me and takes a seat on the opposite end. "I'll be damned if I let you ruin her life a second time."

I grab the mug off the table and take a sip, hoping the warm liquid will help quell the emotions swirling through my entire being. I want to close the space between us and punch him square in the jaw, but that wouldn't solve anything. We aren't kids anymore. Gone are the days when we can throw a few punches, and everything will suddenly go back to normal.

I'll be damned if I sit here and take all the blame for what happened between Emersyn and me. "You're one of my best friends, Beckett. I let you come between us before and ruined any chance of us being together. I spent my entire time overseas reading every email she sent but never responded because I was a coward."

Every email and letter she sent me tore away at my resolve to stay away from her. I knew in my heart that Beckett did the right thing by asking me to wait until I came back from deployment to start anything with her, but it got harder with each passing day. And then she sent me an email confirming my worst fears: She had met someone. She wrote me a very detailed account of a douchebag named Brian. How she turned him down numerous times for dates, but she had given up on waiting for me to tell her how I felt, and she finally agreed. That one night turned into many, and they've been together ever since.

I curled into myself that night, sobbing quietly into my pillow as my heart broke into a million pieces. I got what I wanted. Emersyn was moving on, living the life I always knew she deserved, but with someone other than me. I did this to us, to myself, and I had to bear the consequences of my actions. I tried so hard to be angry with her, to hate her for breaking my heart, but I couldn't. Hell, I can't blame her for moving on.

I spent the better part of a year ignoring her heart-felt emails, filled with well wishes from across the globe and hopes for my safe return. She ended every letter telling me how much she loved and missed me. About how no matter how long it took for me to come home, she'd wait patiently for me to tell her how I felt. But one day, she'd had enough.

"And now it's probably too late, but I have to try. I know she has a boyfriend, but I honestly don't give a fuck," I say with conviction before leaning back onto the couch.

Something I can't place flashes in his eyes but disappears just as quickly. I brace myself for some type of reaction from him, but nothing happens. He just sits there, sipping his coffee with his hazel eyes locked on mine. They scan me, looking for any hint that I might be lying to him, but he isn't going to find one.

"And now you're home. But there's no way I'm going to let you within ten inches of my sister."

I shrug my shoulders, placing the now-lukewarm mug on the table between us. "That's the point, Becks. You don't get a say." I lean forward, resting my forearms on my knees. "I let you get inside my head and twist all my insecurities to your advantage back then, but no more. Emersyn is an adult and can make her own decisions. It's time for both of us to let her start doing that."

I had planned on coming to have a simple conversation, to talk things out and come to an understanding, not pour my heart out to him. However, deep down, I know this needs to happen. If he's expecting me to back down like I did in the past, he has another thing coming. This time, I plan on fighting for Emersyn, taking down anything standing in my way. Including him, if need be.

He places his cup on the coffee table, mirroring my posture. "How is now any different? At the first sign of trouble, you bolted."

"Bolted? I had to go fight a goddamn war, asshole," I growl, my fist clenching against my knees.

"No, you didn't fight me for her. You just took what I said as gospel and walked away without a word."

"Are you fucking kidding me?" I bellow, pushing to my feet and pacing back and forth. "You were my best friend! You knew everything about me. My thoughts. My feelings. How the hell else was I supposed to take your words?"

He sighs loudly. "I was trying to protect my sister."

"From me?" I stop pacing, turning my attention toward him, probably seeing him for the first time since I walked into his apartment.

What I took as calm indifference to me being here is something else entirely. Every muscle in his body seems to be vibrating as if he's forcing himself to remain in place. I'm not sure if it's in anger or something else. His fists clench and unclench on his knees as his head drops toward the floor. I can hear the faint sounds of him mumbling something that I can't make out before he pushes to his feet and storms toward me.

"You broke her heart, asshole. I tried to keep you from hurting her if something happened to you over there, but it happened anyway." His hand shoots out as he grips the collar of my shirt. "The first few weeks after you left, she cried herself to sleep, wondering what she did wrong to make you turn your back on her. Then it turned into months of worrying if you were all right. Thankfully, your mom kept me up to date on what was going on with you, but not hearing from you took its toll."

"I tried to keep my distance, like you said, but it was hard. My resolve broke a little more with each email and package she sent, but then..." I stop as emotions clog my throat.

"It was for the best, Brady. By leaving her, you let her grow and become the woman she is today."

"But I'm home now, for good."

"And?" He raises his eyebrow at me before releasing my collar and taking a step back. "Look, I'm glad you're home, safe and sound, but we've been friends since I was five years old. No one will ever be good enough for her. Not even my best friend."

I shove my hands into my pockets, willing myself to calm down. "I'd never do anything to hurt Emersyn. You can trust me with your sister's heart."

Beckett raises his eyebrow in my direction before shaking his head.

"Okay, poor choice of words." I snicker, holding my hands up in surrender. "I had every intention of telling Emersyn how I felt about her that night."

"I'm sorry, Brady." He sighs before plopping down on the couch beside me. "I was so wrapped up in protecting my baby sister from the world that I'm the one that got in the way of her happiness."

"We both fucked up," I respond, placing my hand on his shoulder. "That's why you're going to help me convince her to break up with her douchebag boyfriend."

"Wait. What douchebag?" Beckett cuts me off.

"The douchebag Emersyn is dating," I respond,

although it shouldn't surprise me that Beckett has no idea Emersyn has a boyfriend.

As overprotective of her as he is, it's a wonder guys can even be within a ten-mile radius of her, let alone date her. However, by the way she was dancing with her boyfriend at the bar last night, I assumed Beckett was aware of his existence and approved. I guess this is what happens when you assume things.

"Emersyn isn't dating anyone," he says with conviction. "If she was dating, I'd know about it."

"Okay, but whether she has a boyfriend or not is irrelevant. You are going to help me convince her to give me another chance."

"Oh, so I'm going to help you, am I?" Beckett chuckles, resting his head on the back of the couch. "I can't promise to help, but this is going to take a little while for me to wrap my head around this. I doubt I'll ever like it, but I won't get in the way anymore."

That's not exactly the answer I was hoping for, but I'll take it. I don't know if my friendship with Beckett will ever be the same, but this is a step in the right direction. He finally understands where I'm coming from.

"Do you mind if I crash on your couch tonight?" I ask, wanting to break the silence.

"Excuse me? Why can't you hang with your buddy, Seth?"

"What are you, jealous?" I snicker, causing Beckett

to scowl in my direction. "I have no desire to be the third wheel." I hold my hand in his direction.

Beckett stares down at my hand for a few moments before giving it a hard shake. "Sorry, man. I missed you, too." He pulls me in for a one-armed man hug as his phone rings loudly.

Beckett quickly releases me before pulling his phone from his pocket and answering. I push to my feet, not wanting to intrude, and grab my half-full cup of coffee and stroll into the kitchen. I take my time washing the cup and placing it on the small drying rack beside the sink.

"That was Sherry. I need to head in so I can sign for the shipment coming in a few hours."

"Ah, okay. I'll get out of your hair."

I move to step around him, but Beckett pulls me in for another warm hug. "I'm glad you're home, Brady. I really am, but if you break her heart again, I'll end you."

"If I break her heart again, you won't have to," I respond with conviction as I pull out of his embrace. "So, can I crash on your couch or not? I really would prefer not to stay with my parents."

Beckett shakes his head. "You got it, man. The spare key is in the same place it's always been. I need to shower and head to the bar."

"Mind if I call Walker and Riggs and see if they want to make the drive to grab some beers?"

"Walker and Riggs spend more time here than in

Rose Hill ever since Mr. Armstrong's health started declining. You could always head over to the restaurant at Tranquility Retreat instead."

Walker Armstrong and Riggs Monroe are the other two people in our friend group. We've all been friends since we were kids, although Riggs didn't come along until high school. While Beckett and I were closest to each other, the same could be said for Walker and Riggs. Although I have a feeling that Riggs was a little more interested in Walker's sister, Leia, than anything else.

"How's he doing, anyway? My mom told me about his last stint in the hospital while I was deployed. I planned on going out to their place just to check in and see how things were going."

"He's doing as well as could be expected for a seventy-something-year-old man who refuses to believe his body is getting older." Beckett runs his hand through his disheveled hair.

Walker's dad grew up on his family farm right outside of Tyson's Creek, but after his parents were married, his mom helped him take things to the next level. It's tucked into the lush and rolling hills just outside of town, but instead of being just a working farm, there's now a warm and inviting inn, spa, and even a rustic farm-to-table restaurant. The story goes that the family farm suffered a drought or something right after Walker's grandfather passed away suddenly from a heart attack, and the family had to survive. It was then that Leia's mom came in with a fresh perspective on things. By turning part of the land into a tourist destination, they could generate revenue for the entire town and save the farm, as well. And the rest is history, as they say.

Now Tranquility Retreat is one of the hottest resort destinations in all of Tennessee. People come from all over the country for a chance to take in the views of the mountains at sunset and learn what it's like to work on a farm at the same time.

"The retreat is booming, but Mr. Armstrong refuses to relinquish any control. He still gets up before the sun to feed the cattle, check the fields, and do all the daily chores that need to be taken care of. Leia has tried a million different things to convince him to take it easy and focus more on the admin side of the business, but he refuses, much to her chagrin."

"Damn. That's tough. Hopefully, they can convince him to retire soon."

"From your mouth to the Lord's ears. But I really need to hop in the shower..."

"Oh shit, right." I reach out and give him a one-arm hug before striding toward the door. "I'll give the guys a call and meet you at Crawdaddy's in about an hour."

"Sounds like a plan," Beckett shouts just as the door swings shut behind me.

Things between Beckett and me seem to be on the

mend, and I may just have an ally in my pursuit of winning Emersyn's heart a second time. All that's left is to come up with the perfect plan to let her know how good we could be together and apologize for being a complete jackass by ignoring her for so long.

That won't be too hard. Will it?

seven
emersyn

"You've got to be kidding me!" I screech as I turn on my car and notice the check engine light on my dashboard.

After pouring my heart out to the girls and downing a copious amount of coffee, along with painkillers, I was hoping the day would be easier. I grabbed a quick shower and planned on grabbing some greasy drive-through food and then passing back out at my parents' house for a few hours before starting my shift at the dance studio. But that would've been too easy.

I turn the car off and send up a silent prayer that my eyes are playing tricks on me before turning it back on. But no such luck.

"What the hell am I going to do?" I mumble to myself as I lean forward, resting my forehead against the steering wheel.

Driving back to my parents' house is out of the question. I wouldn't want to risk driving clear to the other side of town and doing even more damage to my car. Thankfully, Beckett only lives a few miles down the road, and I'm sure he would help me out, but I don't really want a follow-up lecture.

But what other options do I have? The lecture would be far worse if I started toward my parents' house and something happened. I pull my phone out of my jacket pocket and hit the speed dial for Sophie's number.

"You just walked out of my place. What could you possibly want already?" she groans as I hear water running in the background. "I need a shower before I have to people in a few hours."

I giggle softly before groaning as stabbing pain shoots through my head. "My check engine light is on."

"What do you want me to do about that?" I begin to roll my eyes, but the stabbing pain returns. "Can you take me to my parents'?"

"What part of I have to people in a few hours did you not get? I love you, but not that much. Tasha and Rachel are passed out in the spare room again, and I'm standing naked in my bathroom."

"Come on, Soph. I'll owe you."

"You already owe me a million. Call that gorgeous brother of yours. I'm sure he can check it out for you." She yawns loudly into the phone. "Or better yet, call Brady and tell him you lied about having a boyfriend and want to jump his bones."

I open my mouth to respond but close it tightly. I've already decided to tell Brady that I lied about having a boyfriend, but I need more time to figure out what I want to say. He more than likely already thinks I'm unbelievably childish for sending the email in the first place; if I turn around and tell him it was all a lie, I can't imagine him responding well. I just need to find the perfect way to tell him.

"I'm not calling Brady, Soph," I whine, trying to rack my brain for anyone else I could call. "How about you call my brother and tell him to come and check out my car?"

"Tempting, but I want more sleep." Sophie huffs loudly into the phone. "Call Beckett and ask him to take a look at your car. I'm going to shower and then go back to sleep. Love you."

"Love you, too," I respond, but it's too late. She's already hung up. I could call my brother. He only lives a few blocks away from Sophie's house, closer to the center of town, but not by much.

When we were kids, I hated coming to Sophie's. We could never get pizza delivered, and it took almost twenty minutes to get anywhere. But now that I'm older, it's the perfect place to chill and get away from the world. There is something serene in knowing that there isn't another human being for miles, even if the closest person to here I know happens to be my pain-in-the-ass big brother.

I sigh and do the only thing I can in this situation: pull out of the parking lot and head toward my brother's apartment. I arrive just a few minutes later. "Be nice, Em. You need his help, and who knows? He may let you catch a few hours of sleep while he fixes your car." I roll my eyes at myself before climbing out of the car and heading toward Beckett's front door.

I've always tried to find the silver lining in every situation, even when I know there isn't one. I would love to think that when I knock on my brother's door, he'll offer to help me with no questions asked, but in reality, he's going to lecture me about how I need to take better care of my car or whatever bullshit excuse he comes up with this time for not treating me like an adult.

I take a deep breath before plastering a fake smile on my face and knocking. It takes a few moments, but the door flies open, and Beckett stands in front of me in all his glory: a white towel wrapped around his waist and his dark brown hair still wet from the shower he obviously just took. He barely registers my presence before spinning around and heading deeper into the apartment.

I throw my hand over my eyes. "Come on, bro. It's too early for that."

"Early? It's almost one o'clock in the afternoon," he growls before putting his cell phone back to his ear.

Sorry, I mouth toward him before heading into the

living room and taking a seat on his oversized leather couch. The television volume is turned down low, and some action sequence from a video game is playing on the oversized screen. I shake my head. Boys and their toys.

Beckett's one-bedroom apartment isn't anything special, but it's his own. He doesn't have to tell our parents where he's going or when he's coming home. I would give anything for that freedom some days. Sophie and I managed to get paired together as roommates freshman year, and then when we met Rachel and Tasha and moved into a three-bedroom apartment near campus. We don't stay there much, spending all our weekends back here in Tyson's Creek, but it's great to have a place to just be sometimes and not have my parents breathing down my neck, wondering where I am every second of the day.

Don't get me wrong, they text me all the time, wanting to check in and see how things are going. I'm pretty sure they track my location, too, but their being so overbearing is a lot easier to handle when I'm a couple of hours away by car. Going to college so close to home wasn't the plan. I wanted to get as far away from this place as possible when I turned eighteen, but staying near home was the most responsible thing to do.

My parents had just given my brother a large chunk of money to put down as a deposit on his bar, and I didn't want to burden them even more with the worry of paying for my tuition. We aren't hurting for money, but I didn't want to add any stress to them. By going to school near home, I've been able to continue working at the dance studio with Selina here in town and have even started helping Bristol by babysitting little Rebekah for her on days when she needs the extra set of hands. Although it was never my dream to stay here in Tyson's Creek, I can't complain.

I'd be lying to myself if I didn't acknowledge the small part of me that wanted to stay close to town for when Brady came home. He made it perfectly clear by ignoring all my emails and letters while he was deployed that he wanted nothing more to do with me and he regretted the moment we shared before he left, but I had to know. I needed to see with my own eyes that he was home, safe and sound.

"To what do I owe this pleasure, Em?" Beckett ruffles my hair before plopping down on the couch beside me, thankfully now fully clothed in a pair of jeans and a long-sleeved Henley shirt.

"The check engine light came on in my car this morning." I immediately hold my hand in front of his face. "I don't need a lecture. My head is killing me, and I've got to be at the dance studio by four. Can you look at it for me?"

"Sure thing, but I don't know how much work I can get done on it before I have to head into the bar." He pushes off the couch and heads toward the small closet between his bedroom and the kitchen.

"You own a bar. Why the hell are you going in before five p.m.?" I whine like a brat, following closely behind him. I just want to get my car fixed and get some sleep.

"There are other things to do besides serve you and your friends alcohol." He crouches down and begins searching for something in the closet. "Sherry's son is sick, so I have to go sign for the shipment coming in, take inventory, and make sure everything is ready to open in a few hours."

"Wait. Does that mean you have to work again tonight?" I ask, trying to make sense of what he isn't saying.

"Yes. Being the boss means extra responsibility. I can't just blow things off because I'm tired," he says as he reaches for a bag in the closet and stands, heading toward the front door. "Let's check out your car."

"I'm sorry, Becks. I'm hungover and being a brat." I wrap my arms around his waist and squeeze. "I had no idea you had to work so hard to keep the bar going."

"There are a lot of things you have no idea about, Emersyn," he responds softly before planting a kiss on the top of my head, pulling the door open, and striding toward my car.

"What the hell is that supposed to mean?" I jog

quickly past him, unlock my car, and pop the hood for him.

"You know nothing of the world but Tyson's Creek. You've never been to more than a handful of states in your entire life. You've been anchoring yourself here. It's my job to protect you."

"Fuck you, Beckett." My eyes fill with tears as my brother's true feelings finally come to the surface. "Is that how you see me? A little girl who needs protecting from the big, bad world?"

"That's not what I said, Emersyn." He sighs as he leans under the hood of my car and starts fiddling around with something.

"Maybe not, but that's exactly what you meant," I shout, throwing my arms in the air. "You're right. I haven't seen much of the world. But Brady has nothing to do with that."

Beckett and I both know that's a lie, but I won't give him the satisfaction of saying it out loud. Brady may be part of the reason I chose to stay close to home, but he wasn't the only one.

"I could have gone to the other side of the country for college, but I decided to stay home. For you and our parents."

"What's that supposed to mean?" Beckett stands to his full height, crossing his arms and leaning against the front end of my car.

"It means that our parents had just given you a

large-ass sum of money to buy Crawdaddy's, so I decided to stay close to ease the burden on them financially and be here to support you if you needed me. Do you honestly think I come home every weekend and drink at your bar for the fun of it?"

"I thought it was for the free drinks." He scoffs, turning his head away from me and staring into space.

"You choose to give us the free drinks, but I can guarantee you've noticed the wads of cash left in the tip jar after we leave." I huff, leaning on the car beside him. "I know it makes you feel better to have all of us close so you can watch over us. I mean, it might also have a little to do with your crush on my best friend."

"It's my job to protect you from all the bad things in the world. And I don't..." he begins, but I cut him off.

"Did you stop to think that I might enjoy going to college close to home? That I may feel better to know that I have someplace safe to be me and not worry about how others might react to me? There is something to be said about knowing that the next person coming around the corner isn't out to get me."

"I'm sorry." Beckett wraps his arms around my shoulder, pulling me to his side. "I know in my heart you're old enough to take care of yourself, as someone reminded me recently, but it's hard not to be your big brother sometimes. I can't stop the feeling that I need to protect you from being hurt by the outside world."

"And who reminded you that I'm not a little girl anymore?" I whisper, hope flickering in my chest.

"The same person who came to my place this morning to ask me to help break up you and this mysterious boyfriend I've never heard of."

My cheeks instantly heat as I try to come up with an explanation that Beckett will believe. I've always been a horrible liar, but I can't exactly tell him I made it up. Can I? There is no way I would ever live down that embarrassment.

"I don't know who you're talking about, Becks." I snort, looking anywhere but at him.

"So you don't have a boyfriend?" he asks, leaning down slightly so he can look me in the eye.

We stare at each other in silence for a few moments before he bursts out in laughter. "Oh man, Em. You made up a boyfriend to make him jealous, didn't you?"

"Not one of my finer moments, but yeah. I guess I did." I mumble, crossing my arm over my chest.

I. Am. Mortified. I would be so grateful if the ground would open up and swallow me whole right this instant. But when that doesn't happen, I turn to make my brother. Might as well get this over with now.

"So, what are you going to do with this information?"

"Absolutely nothing. Whatever outcome you planned by telling him you were seeing someone, it worked." He scoffs before turning around and fiddling under the hood of my car again. "I got between the two of you once, but I won't do it again. He fucked up, and he knows it, but it's up to you whether you want to forgive him or not."

My breath hitches at the idea that Brady came to talk to Beckett. I know their friendship hasn't been the same since Beckett saw the two of us kissing before Brady left for deployment. It makes sense that Brady would want to find a way to bury the hatchet when he came home. But what does that have to do with me? It makes perfect sense that they'd talk about me, even if it was in passing. Even though I know all these things, my heart races inside my chest, wondering in what context my name came up between these two. Did Brady come to apologize for ignoring me for two years and breaking my heart, or did he tell Beckett it was a mistake to kiss me in the first place? Damn, do I wish it was the first one, but I can't get my hopes up. Brady had more than one opportunity to get in contact with me while he was deployed, but he didn't use one of them. Although, there are a million reasons why he didn't contact me. Especially after I pulled such a childish stunt. No, I can't let my mind go there.

"He did fuck up. Royally," I respond softly, my mind continuing to race with different scenarios.

"That's my girl. I did warn him that if he hurts you a second time, he won't live through it."

"Beckett." I giggle, slapping him hard on the shoulder. "You do know that I don't need protection from Brady or anyone else. I'm an adult, whether you like it or not. I'll make mistakes—many of them, in fact—but what I need to know is that my big brother will be there for me when I need him. Not as a protector, but as a friend."

He rolls his eyes as he stands up, slamming the hood of my car shut in the process. "I hear what you're saying, but it's going to take a while to turn off my big brother tendencies and see you as anything other than the little pink bundle our parents brought home when I was seventeen years old."

"All I'm asking is for you to try. Rome wasn't built in a day." I smile before shoving my hands into the pockets of my shorts. "So what's the verdict?"

"I have absolutely no idea." My eyes widen in surprise as he snickers softly. "But don't worry, Em. Your car will be as good as new before tonight."

"How?"

"Don't you worry your pretty little head." He plants a kiss on my forehead before striding toward his car. "When have I ever let you down?"

"Never."

"Exactly. Now hop in my car. I'll give you a ride to Mom and Dad's. The shipment should be arriving any minute now, so I need to head out."

I want to whine and complain about depending on my parents for a ride, but the last thing Beckett needs is for me to be a brat right now. Sure, my mom can't be on time to save her soul, even with a million alarms. I'll just make sure to shoot Selina a text to let her know I'll probably be running about fifteen minutes late. With almost three hours' notice, I doubt she'll be too pissed at me.

"Okay, but can we stop for food? I doubt they have anything in the house that will help with this hangover."

"I'll stop at Culver's on the way. Sound good?"

"Always." I giggle before wrapping my arms around Beckett's waist and giving him a tight squeeze. "You're the best, big brother."

"I'd do anything for you, Emersyn. All you have to do is ask." He plants a kiss on the top of my head before pulling out of my grasp and heading toward his car.

I want to beg him to make Brady talk to me. There's a strong possibility that he wants nothing to do with me, but the least he can do is explain what changed the minute I left him alone with Beckett that night. I deserve that, at the very least. Then I can put this whole thing behind me and try to move on.

Yeah, right. Who am I kidding? There is no moving on from a guy like Brady. It's more like coping with the fact that he doesn't want anything to do with me.

Now, let's just hope whatever he has to say doesn't shatter my heart into a million pieces.

eight
brady

After leaving Beckett's apartment, I headed back to my place to grab a change of clothes and a toothbrush. Thankfully, Seth was in the shower, and I didn't interrupt his special night with Bristol. I wished him good luck a second time and dropped into my parents' house to give my mom another kiss before hopping back into my truck and heading toward Tranquility Retreat.

I know I said I was going to call Walker and Riggs, but I haven't been to the property in ages, and I might be trying to run into Walker's sister, Leia, to get the inside scoop on what's been going on with Bristol since Seth and I left on deployment.

My boy called Bristol every chance he got while we were deployed, but she never answered. He also never left a message, so there's that, but I want to know what Seth is walking into. I doubt Bristol would've agreed to dinner with him if she was in a relationship, but a lot of things can change in a year.

I rub my hand over the ache in my chest as I pull into the long drive leading to the Armstrongs' farmhouse, tucked into the corner of the property, and park right in front.

The house has a large covered wraparound porch that takes up almost the entire front of the house, with a porch swing positioned to give you the perfect view of the sun setting over the mountains when you sit there. It's a warm butter yellow color with white framed windows practically covering the front of it and a manicured garden with perfectly trimmed bushes and a bright array of flowers, which gives it an even more welcoming feel.

"As I live and breathe, look what the cat dragged in." Leia's sing-song voice filters through my open windows, causing me to smile brightly. I climb out of the car and stride towards her, hopping up onto the porch with little effort before wrapping her in a tight hug. Leia giggles softly as I twirl her around in a circle and plant her feet safely back on the ground. "Hey, Leia."

Yes, Walker's younger sister's name is Leia. After Princess Leia from *Star Wars*, and the youngest Armstrong sibling is named Skye. I don't know the entire story, but their mom came to Tyson's Creek to see some comet or something and never left. Their parents met when their mom was on that trip, and the rest is history.

"Hey, Brady. So glad you're here," she responds with a smile of her own as I take a step back and take a good at her.

She looks almost the same as she did before I left. Leia is a few inches taller than me, her blonde hair hanging in loose curls down her back over the pastel pink sweater that says *Favorite Auntie* scrolled in an elegant script across the front. She's wearing a pair of grey pants that fit tightly to her body. Her wire-frame glasses are perched on the end of her nose, and thick black eyelashes frame her crystal blue eyes, which are shining with excitement.

"Auntie? Did Walker finally decide to settle down and start a family?"

"Oh, hell no." She giggles, her eyes instantly dropping to the ground as she fiddles with the edge of her shirt. "Selina and Vance are having a baby."

"I just saw Vance last night at Crawdaddy's, and he couldn't stop gushing about being a daddy. I'm glad those two found their way back to each other," I respond. It's not a complete lie but not the whole truth either.

My mind has been so preoccupied with my meeting with Emersyn last night that I completely forgot that Vance and Selina are expecting their first child together. Before I left on deployment, Vance was still head over heels in love with his high school sweetheart, Selina Grymes. She left without saying goodbye to anyone and headed off to Juilliard and never looked back. It seems a lot of things have changed for the better. Hope flares inside my chest, but I quickly tamp it down. Vance and Selina had a long history of love between them when she left for New York, and I doubt the story of them finding their way back to each other was all sunshine and rainbows. But one can hope.

"Oh, I know all about your trip to Crawdaddy's last night." Leia giggles, crossing her arms over her chest and eyeing me skeptically.

"I have no idea what you're talking about," I respond, feigning ignorance, but she isn't having any of it.

"Uh-huh, just like there's nothing more than friendship between you and Emersyn."

"Touché." I snort, throwing my arm over her shoulder and heading toward the front door. "Now, what can you tell me about a certain redheaded best friend of yours?"

"You came all the way out here just to get the inside scoop for your friend?" she questions as she grabs the screen door and swings it open.

"No, I came to ask your brother and Riggs to have a beer with me at Crawdaddy's while I try to hatch a plan on how to break up Emersyn and her boyfriend while simultaneously convincing her that we are destined to be together. You being here to give me the scoop on Bristol is just a bonus."

Bristol and Leia have been friends since being paired together for a project during college. Instead of going home after graduation, Bristol decided to come back to Tyson's Creek with Leia. I'm not sure if she planned to make a career out of teaching yoga, but she opened Nurture Space a few months before we left on deployment. That's how she and Seth met for the first time. Walker had asked if we could come to a mock class so she could complete her training hours for her certification, and the rest is history. Seth was smitten with her at first sight, although the feeling was anything but mutual. However, Seth managed to bring down the walls surrounding Bristol's heart shortly before we left. Hopefully, he has an easier time this go-around.

I probably didn't need to tell her my entire plan and instead simply said yes to her question, but I need all the help I can get at this point. Proving how sorry I am to Emersyn while also breaking up her relationship isn't going to be easy by any means, but I'm up for the challenge.

"Hmmm," Leia responds as we step through the door and right into the main portion of the house.

There is no entryway to this house, just a great room filled with cozy-looking furniture and a grand fireplace tucked into the back of the room. I notice Riggs and Walker sitting on a cream-colored loveseat positioned near the fireplace, across from Mr. Armstong. Riggs notices me immediately and says something to

Walker before pushing to his feet and heading toward Leia and me.

His eyes remain locked on her, and a smirk spreads across his face as he strolls toward us. To anyone else who didn't know him, you'd believe he was completely relaxed. His right hand is shoved into the front pocket of his dark-colored jeans as he runs his free hand through his hair. The long sleeves of his light blue button-up shirt are rolled to the elbows and tucked into the waistband of his pants. But most wouldn't notice the way his fist tightens into a ball as he notices my arm thrown over Leia's shoulder or the rage burning in his eyes as they narrow slightly in my direction before it quickly disappears, and he throws a wink in Leia's direction.

"I'll leave you to it, then," Leia says quickly, her cheeks turning a light shade of pink, as she ducks out from beneath my arm.

She smiles brightly at me before heading to a different part of the house, but I grab her hand. "You aren't gonna tell me anything?"

"Emersyn has to work at the dance studio this afternoon." Leia's eyebrows pull down in confusion.

"Thanks for that, but I mean about Bristol."

"No," she deadpans, pulling her hand free from my grasp. "If your best friend wants to get closer to my best friend, he's gonna have to do it the old-fashioned way." Without another word, she spins on her heels and heads toward the offices situated on the opposite side of the house.

"That woman works entirely too much. If she isn't careful, she's going to have nothing left to give anyone, let alone this business," Riggs says from beside me, his eyes locked on Leia's retreating form.

It's a mystery to all of us what happened between those two when we were younger. They went from being thick as thieves to hating each other overnight. Hate is too strong of a word for what goes on between them, but there is something. We've all speculated over the years, and I've even outright asked Riggs before, but he usually changes the subject quickly. I have a sneaking suspicion that Riggs and I are in a similar situation. Walker and Riggs are just as close, if not closer, than Beckett and I were before he walked out on Emersyn and me kissing. I can only imagine what would happen if Walker caught Riggs in such a compromising position. He isn't nearly as protective of his sisters as Beckett is of Emersyn, but I doubt it would go over well.

Either way, anyone who spent time with those two knew there was something more than friendship between them, but one day, the summer before they went off to college and I joined the Marines, Leia made sure to put as much distance between the two of them as possible. She stopped tagging along with us on trips to the river and camping under the stars on the property. It was like she was hiding away from all of us. She was always nice to me whenever I saw her around their property or out in town. But the moment Riggs opened his mouth, the temperature in the room would drop. I haven't seen much of them together since then, but the way he feels about her is written all over his face right now.

"When are you going to tell her how you feel about her, Riggs?" I say, throwing my arm over his shoulder and pulling him in for a one-armed hug.

"The same time you say something to Emersyn."

"You better get ready." I wink before removing my arm and heading into the living room to join Walker and Mr. Armstrong.

Walker pushes to his feet as soon as he sees me coming and pulls me into a warm hug. His muscular arms wrap tightly around my shoulder as he slaps me hard on the back before pulling away. "So good to have you home, Brady."

A blinding smile spreads across his face, his soulful cerulean blue eyes shining with happiness. Just like everyone else, Walker looks almost the same as he did before I left. The only difference is a few grey hairs littering the sides of his dark hair, not that I plan on pointing those out, and a thick black beard that covers his jawline.

"It's good to be home, man." I step out of his embrace, turning toward Mr. Armstong. "How are you feeling? My mom told me about your recent visit to the hospital."

I lean down, wrapping my arm around his shoulder and hugging him softly. If I didn't know about all the health problems he's been having, I'd think he was perfectly fine, other than the small canister of oxygen sitting on the floor beside the couch and the clear tubing affixed to his face. My eyes flick to Walker, wanting to ask him about this new development, but he shakes his head. Mr. Armstrong has always been a proud man, and stubborn to boot. I have no doubt that if I mention the oxygen tank, it will disappear the moment we walk out of the room.

"Nothing I can't handle." He coughs before narrowing his eyes at Walker. "But I'd finally be able to enjoy old age and retire if this son of mine would come home and take over the business."

"Pops, I've told you a million times already. My life is in Rose Hill. Besides, you have Leia here. What do you need me here for? I'd only be in the way."

Mr. Armstrong has been pressuring Walker to come home and take over Tranquility Retreat since he graduated from college. It seems it's the Armstrong family tradition to pass the farm to the oldest male family member, but the only problem is Walker wants nothing to do with it. He's made it clear, on numerous occasions, that he's always wanted a life for himself outside of this town. That's one of the many reasons he and Riggs moved to Rose Hill after graduation and joined the fire department. Walker has managed to work his way up to fire chief during that time, while Riggs is happy right where he is.

When Mr. Armstrong's health started declining a little over a year ago, he became more insistent about Walker coming home to take over the business while completely ignoring everything Leia has done to keep this place running since returning home after college. Walker is more than happy to let her take over the family business, but Mr. Walker isn't having it.

"That's not how we do things, Walker, and you know it."

"Well, maybe it's time for things to change, Pops," Walker snaps back before sighing softly.

"Back to your respective corners, gentleman." Riggs smiles, pretending to step between the two men and separate them. "Besides, you're not going anywhere any time soon, Mr. A."

"Yeah. Yeah. Because heaven doesn't want me, and hell's afraid I'll take over." He chuckles while shaking his head, his eyes slowly drooping. "Only you could turn death into a joke."

"It's not a joke; it's the truth." Riggs winks before motioning over his shoulder toward the French doors leading to the deck. "We're gonna head outside and chat. Holler if you need anything."

"I'll be here," Mr. Armstrong responds before he leans his head back and allows his eyes to close.

The three of us don't say a word as we quietly open the doors and slide outside. The moment the doors are shut behind us, Walker states the obvious. "He's getting worse."

"How bad it is?" I ask, not wanting to pry but worried about his declining health. "It's been a while since I last saw him, but he looks so much worse than before I left."

"He is, and we have no idea why. He refuses to let any of us come to appointments with him, and he won't let the doctor give us any information," Walker responds as we stare at the beautiful scenery surrounding the Armstrongs' home.

"Is there anything you can do?" I question, at a loss for what else to say.

"No. He's still of sound mind, so short of him being deemed incompetent in court, there isn't anything we can do but hope he's telling us the truth."

"And what is he telling you?"

"That he's old, and the doctor wants him to slow down," Riggs responds, sliding between Walker and me and leaning his arms on the railing. "Which means he's riding Walker's ass even more than before."

I have no experience with family members being sick, but I do know a lot about loss. Not all my friends made it back from every deployment. I'd like to say I'm desensitized to it by this point, but I'm not. To be honest, I've been even more cognizant of how little control we have over our own safety when on deployment than I did before. Beckett threw the chance that I might not come home in my face that night, and it hit its mark. I didn't want Emersyn sitting by the phone, waiting for a phone call that something happened to me. I didn't want her to feel the pain of losing someone she loved, so I took his advice and stayed away. But now I'm home, and the only thing standing in my way of getting my girl is a boyfriend. But he should be easy enough to get rid of.

"So, enough about my dad. What did you come here to talk about?"

"Can't I just come and visit two of my oldest friends?" I respond, reaching up and rubbing the back of my head with my hand.

I meant what I said when I told Leia I wanted advice about how to win over Emersyn, but now that I've seen Mr. Armstrong for myself, it doesn't seem right to bring it up. I could ask them to head over to Crawdaddy's to grab a beer, and we can talk about it there, but even that seems inappropriate right now.

"You could, but I have a feeling that's not why you came," Walker responds, not bothering to look in my direction.

"Cut the crap, Walker." Riggs chuffs him on the back of the head before turning toward me. "Beckett texted me and said you guys chatted about Emersyn. Since I doubt he was any help other than to promise not to bite your head off anymore, you came for some advice."

"Yeah." I snicker. "She has a boyfriend, and I need to break them up, apologize for being a complete dick and ignoring her, and tell her that she's the love of my life and that we belong together."

"Nothing too hard." Walker chuckles before turning around to lean his back on the railing.

"Yeah, tell me about it."

"This conversation is definitely going to require some beers," Riggs replies before heading toward the opposite end of the deck and through the back door leading into the kitchen.

"I really hope he doesn't give my sister a hard time for once. She's been on edge since this morning."

"That might be because Seth ran into Bristol this morning."

"You don't say." His eyes narrow slightly before he plasters a fake smile onto his face. "I hope those two can sort out their shit this time."

"Me, too. Seth is over the moon for Bristol and deserves a chance to be happy with the person he loves."

"It's that serious between those two?"

"Yes. He retired and moved his entire life here to have a chance to be with her long term."

Seth and Bristol have been doing this dance around each other since the moment they met, and he's hinted at wanting something permanent between them on more than one occasion. It wasn't that far out of the realm of possibilities that he would move here after retirement. Sure, my parents and I are the closest thing has to family, but Bristol is his main reason for coming back here. If it weren't for her, I doubt he'd have even retired.

"You were out of beer, but I managed to swipe a bottle of whiskey from the cabinet in your dad's office." Riggs holds up the carafe and three glasses in the other hand before coming to a stop in front of us.

"Isn't it a little early for whiskey?" I question, glancing at my watch. "It's only a little after one in the afternoon."

"It's never too early for whiskey."

"We both know you just brought beer over last night. You grabbed the whiskey because you wanted to go into the office and bother my sister." Walker smirks, grabbing two of the glasses from him before handing one to me.

"Guilty as charged. I can't resist pushing her buttons."

"We aren't kids anymore, Riggs. Just tell her how you feel, or leave her alone."

Walker and Riggs stare at each other for a few moments. It's as if they're having a silent conversation with each other before Riggs breaks eye contact with a shake of his head. "Enough chatting, time for drinking."

Riggs pours each of us a finger of whiskey before pulling one of the Adirondack chairs closer to us and taking a seat. "Okay. Speak."

I shake my head at one of my best friends as I take a sip from the glass. The liquid warms my chest as I try and figure out where to start explaining things to them. "Long story short, Emersyn told me she loved me before I left for deployment."

"And what did you say?" Walker questions, swirling the liquid around in his glass before taking a healthy pull.

"Nothing. We kissed, and then Beckett walked out and caught us. I let him get into my head, and I left without saying anything to her."

"Okay. That isn't too bad. Just tell her you're an asshole and you love her. Then you can spend the rest of your life making it up to her." Riggs raises his glass in a mock toast before taking a drink.

"It's not that easy at all," I respond with a shake of my head, my eyes focusing on the rolling hills in the distance. "I also ignored every email, letter, and package she has sent me while I was away."

"Fuck," they respond in unison.

"Exactly."

"And you said something about a boyfriend?" Riggs questions.

I nod. "She told me in one of her last emails. I also saw them dancing with each other at Crawdaddy's last night. It took everything in me not to beat the little punk's face in."

"I doubt that would've gone over well." Riggs says, taking another healthy pull from his glass. "But can I ask an obvious question?" I nod my head, waiting for him to continue. "Do you know how she feels?"

"Yes. No. Maybe." I pause to take a large gulp of whiskey, wincing at the burn as it travels down my throat. "There was something there when we saw each other last night. A spark of what was there before I left, but I don't know for sure. I wasn't in a position to ask her."

"Okay, let's table that part for a minute," Walker responds, resting his glass on the railing. "Why the fuck have you ignored her? It would've been easy enough to respond to an email. I know telling her how you feel in a letter or email isn't ideal, but you could've at least responded to her."

"Like I said, I let Beckett get into my head. I was convinced that I wasn't good enough for her and needed to give her a chance to live her life instead of tying her to me. I could've lost my life over there, and I refused to do that to her. So, I went back to my original plan to tell her how I felt when I came home and got my shit together. I wanted to make sure I was able to give her the life she deserved."

"And who are you to decide what someone deserves?" Walker crosses his arms over his chest, his eyes switching between Riggs and me. I guess the two of us have more in common than I originally thought. The only difference is Walker seems to be all for Riggs having a relationship with Leia, the exact opposite of how Beckett was. Things between Beckett and me might be on the mend, but I can't foresee him being okay with Emersyn and me being together anytime soon. At this point, he's barely tolerating the idea that I want to be in a relationship with his sister; asking for anything more would be pushing my luck for sure.

"You don't understand. You have a career, a college degree, and stability. Exactly what a woman like Emersyn desires in a man she wants to spend the rest of her life with." I stroll past Riggs and take a seat in the nearest chair. "With my military salary, I barely made enough to save any money, let alone enough to buy a house here in town. Fuck, I stayed in this long for the retirement to ensure I had money coming in. I live above my parents' garage, rent-free, and my job with Ace & Hammer pays enough to cover my half of the bills, but doesn't leave much for anything else."

Riggs shrugs his shoulder. "So what?"

"What the fuck is that supposed to mean?"

"It means no one has their shit together." Riggs throws back the remaining bit of liquid in his glass before pouring another. "Walker has a job and a house, but that's it. I can't even tell you the last time he did anything besides work or come back to Tyson's Creek to visit his dad."

"And Riggs lives in my house, works for me, and refuses to grow a set and tell my sister he's in love with her because of something he said when he was sixteen years old," Walker responds immediately, taking another sip of his half-full glass.

"I sense a story there," I respond, my head swiveling between my two friends.

"There is, but that's not what we are talking about." Riggs places his glass on the deck before turning toward me in his chair. "From where I'm standing, you and Emersyn are in limbo, and limbo means you need to make a decision."

My blood boils as images of that douchebag touching her last night flood my mind. The idea of him caressing her soft skin, her luscious lips pressed against his in a passionate kiss, or her moaning in pleasure for someone else other than me, makes me want to vomit the meager contents of my stomach all over the floor. "I have made a decision; that's why I'm here. But I'd be lying if I said I was sure this would work out. Ever since my going away party, I've been waiting for the day she realizes she can do better than me—much better. She moved on and found someone else. It is possible that the spark I thought I saw between us last night was a figment of my imagination. It'd kill me, but

I'd let her go. The only thing I want for her is to be happy."

"Then, I guess the first thing you need to do is ask her." Riggs raises the carafe of whiskey, asking if I want more, but I shake my head no.

"Ask her if she still cares about me?"

"Yes, and about this boyfriend of hers."

"I don't need to ask about the boyfriend. She told me..." My voice trails off as I think back to last night.

Yes, Emersyn told me in her email that she had a boyfriend, but I watched her almost the entire night. Creepy, I know, but that's beside the point. Other than dancing with him for that short period of time, she spent most of her time with Sophie and two other girls I'd never met before. They danced together, spent time at the bar, and they even all left together. Not once did I see her with a guy. Could I be reading too much into the dance? Maybe, but it's possible that the boyfriend wasn't there last night, right?

"I can see the wheels turning in your head." Walker strides toward me before gripping my shoulder, giving it a squeeze to get my attention. "People lie. It stands to reason that Emersyn could've lied to you about being in a relationship to make you jealous."

My eyebrows pull down in confusion as I try to make some sense of what he said.

I open my mouth to respond, but he cuts me off. "Attention is attention. Even the negative kind. You were ignoring her. What better way to get your attention than by making you jealous?"

"I don't know Emersyn well, but the only thing most women want is for someone to love and cherish them. Everything else is window dressing."

I ponder what he's saying for a minute. Emersyn never asked me for anything in her emails besides the standard *come home safely,* which everyone in my life asked for. She also repeated in every email and letter that she would wait for me. That she wasn't breakable, and she could handle anything life threw our way. But I didn't listen to what she was telling me. I was so worried about what I wanted and what I thought was best for her that I made decisions without her. I didn't respond to the emails because I was scared of exactly what happened, that she'd get tired of waiting. But did she really? I pushed her away and made her feel like I didn't feel the same way for her that she did for me.

It's as if a light bulb has gone off in my head. I was so worried about protecting her that I broke her instead. I've been holding Emersyn on a pedestal, just like Beckett, but I wasn't protecting her; I was protecting myself from the pain of being rejected. I've always believed Emersyn deserved someone better than me and that my love for her wouldn't be enough. I didn't want to put my heart on the line, only to find out that she may not love me as I loved her. So, I ran. Yeah, Beckett added fuel to the fire with all the things he said, and he had valid points. Yes, she's only in her early twenties, but she knows what she wants. And that is me. She didn't ask for anything else in return but my love. "Fuck. How do I do this?"

"First, you need to stop straddling the fence with her. Either you want to be with her, or you don't. There is no halfway because you won't get another chance after this."

I turn and meet my friend's eyes and see nothing but sincerity. "I'm afraid of what it will do to me if she tells me to fuck off."

"I understand, but you can't keep planning for her to leave you. Instead, work on giving her a reason to stay," Riggs responds with conviction.

"Pot, meet kettle," Walker grumbles.

"Again, we aren't talking about me," Riggs snaps back before pushing to his feet and storming through the French doors leading into the living room.

"For someone who gives such good advice on getting back into the good graces of the woman I love, he sure is clueless."

"Tell me about it." Walker shakes his head before plopping down in Riggs's vacant seat. "Leia and Riggs are in love with each other; anyone with eyes can see that. The problem is that my sister is stubborn, and the walls she has around her heart are so thick I don't even know if anyone will be able to get through."

"Even Riggs?"

"If anyone has a chance at breaking through them, it's Riggs," Walker responds as the shrill ring of my cell phone rings.

I pull it quickly from my pocket and notice Beckett's name lighting the screen. "It's Beckett."

Walker nods his head as he pushes to his feet. "I'm going to go check on my dad. If you still want to grab that beer, let me know."

"Will do," I respond before answering the call.

"Hello."

"What do you know about cars?" Beckett spits out, getting right to the point.

"Enough to get by. We did a lot of our own maintenance in the sandbox. I wouldn't say I'm an expert, but I know how to fix the basics," I respond, trying to figure out where he's going with this.

Beckett is silent for a few moments before I hear him sigh loudly. "I know I said I wasn't going to help you get with my sister, but she came by before I left for the bar and needs some help with her car. The check engine light came on, and she has to head to work in a few hours. Can you go take a look at it?"

"Sure," I say, a goofy smile spreading across my face. "I was just leaving Walker's dad's place. I'll head right over there and take a look at it."

"She isn't there," he deadpans, and my smile immediately falls. "But she does have to work at the dance studio later today. The keys are in the visor on the driver's side. You can take it over to her once it's fixed."

"Sounds like a plan," I respond before saying goodbye.

It might not be what I had in mind of how to get Emersyn to speak to me, but this is a step in the right direction. Barre Studio is a neutral location and the perfect place to have a conversation. I can ask her about her boyfriend and figure out if there's any part of her that still loves me, no matter how small. Then I can put *Operation Win Emersyn's Heart* into action.

With a plan slowly forming in my mind, I head inside to say goodbye to everyone.

I have work to do.

nine
brady

After saying my goodbyes to everyone at Tranquility Retreat, I head right to Beckett's apartment to take a look at Emersyn's car. Thankfully, I keep a small tool kit under the bench of my truck for emergencies. When I arrive, I easily find the keys tucked into the visor and pop the hood. After a quick check of some wires and a few other things, I find the problem before heading to the auto parts store to grab everything I need.

The moment I get back to Beckett's, I get to work, needing something to focus my attention on so I can think through everything going on in my head. With each turn of the wrench, things become even clearer.

The emails. I can't really do anything about the letters, although I still have all of them tucked away in a box under my bed. It would take too long for me to get my answers to her. However, the emails are quick and easy. She deserves a response to each and every one of them, telling her how much I missed her and how she filled every one of my dreams. She needs to hear that I came back home safely to her and that there was nowhere else I'd rather be in this world than with her because I'm completely and utterly in love with her.

But first, I need to talk to her. I need to know if she really is in a relationship. If she is, I want to know if she's happy. I meant what I said to Riggs and Walker a few hours ago. The only thing I've ever wanted is for Emersyn to be happy, even if that means we aren't together. I can stand by and wait for this asshole to mess up, because he will, and then I can set the second part of my plan in motion. Either way, Emersyn deserves to know how I feel because I've kept her waiting long enough.

It's only been a day since I saw her again for the first time, and my heart aches like someone has ripped it out of my chest. Until that moment, I didn't fully understand Seth's issue with Bristol giving him the cold shoulder and not responding to his texts or calls, but now I understand. Seth has longed to know her. To learn all the small tidbits of Bristol's life that he's missed while they've been apart. He's like a kid on Christmas morning, waiting for the next little piece of herself she is willing to share with him. I have a feeling that it will take some time, but today is the first time they've seen each other since we got back from deployment. I know in my heart that, with time, those two will continue getting closer to each other. The worst part is I had that and was too pigheaded to realize it.

But I hope that there is a part of Emersyn that is willing to allow me to prove to her we can be that way again. That the man who ran away from her two years ago isn't the man I am today. I won't let anyone get between us, not her brother, my job, nothing. I've let her brother get to me in the past, creating doubt in my mind, telling me I wasn't good enough for her and that I didn't even deserve to breathe the same air as her. And I know he was right, but that doesn't mean I can't spend the rest of my life making it up to her.

Once I finish fixing Emersyn's car, I climb in and head toward downtown, although downtown Tyson's Creek really isn't anything to write home about. It's one street going through the center of town, leading to the covered bridge and Tranquility Retreat on the other side of the river.

Rustic-looking buildings line the road as I inch closer to the center of town. The streets are lined with people, but no one is rushing around or in a hurry to get anywhere. Tyson's Creek looks exactly like what you'd envision a small, southern town being. There are a few mom-and-pop shops lining the street and no major chain stores in sight. As I drive downtown, I see The Flickhouse, the small movie theater we used to go to as kids, sitting on one corner. There's a small bookstore tucked right next to it, with Tyson's Hardware on the other side. Across the street from the theater is Just the Drip, a coffee shop-bakery combo, which has a few tables out front, with peach-colored umbrellas open, casting shade over each table to protect the occupants from the spring sun. Right next to it is Bristol's yoga studio, Nurture Space, and the dance studio is a few shops down.

I pull into a spot between the two businesses, not wanting to give Emersyn's surprise away, and hop out. I take a deep breath to calm my nerves before striding toward the entrance to Barre Studio and walking right in.

Emersyn is tucked behind the small welcome table in the right-hand corner of the room. To the left, along the outer wall, are two sets of metal lockers Selina had us install during the remodel. The top two rows of lockers have nameplates with the older dancers' names on them and a lock, giving them space to keep some things at the studio and not have to bring them every day. The other lockers aren't assigned to anyone, giving the younger dancers places to store their dance bags during class. There are comfortable chairs scattered around the room for parents to sit and wait for their dancers to finish class. On the other wall, running behind the welcome area, there are bright-colored leotards, bags, and photos of ballet dancers scattered along the wall to the right of the desk, stopping just short of the door leading into the dance space.

"Brady?" she whispers, her eyes widening slightly as she steps around the desk. "What are you doing here?"

"I came to deliver your car." I smile brightly at her, raising her keys to eye level and shaking them slightly. "Beckett asked me to take a look at it for him since he had to run to work."

"Thank you, but you didn't need to do that."

"I know." The air crackles between us as I stare into her eyes. "But I wanted an excuse to see you."

I can't stop my eyes from roaming down her body. Her pert nipples peek through the leotard material that she's wearing, showing off all her ample curves and sheer pink skirt tied neatly at her waist.

"Up here."

My eyes snap up to her, and I smile. No sense in trying to hide the fact that I was checking her out. "I would apologize, but I'm not sorry."

We both chuckle softly before she gets down to business. "I hope there wasn't anything too serious with my car. I always get worried when the check engine light comes on."

"Coming from your boyfriend's place? I hope you didn't drive too far like that," I say nonchalantly, trying to find the perfect segue to ask her about this mysterious boyfriend.

It's logical for me to assume that she didn't stay the night at Beckett's place last night since she wasn't there when I arrived, so that only leaves her parents', Sophie's, or her boyfriend's place. There's no way Beckett would've let her head back to college after drinking so much. Her parents' house is an option, but I doubt she'd want to subject herself to the third degree she'd get from them by coming home drunk. So that leaves Sophie's or the douchebag's.

"My boyfriend's place?" she questions, her head cocked to the side for a moment before her cheeks pink slightly. "No, I was coming from Sophie's place."

Not exactly the answer I was searching for, but I'll take it. "How is Sophie, by the way? Still pining after your brother?"

Peals of laughter escape her lips. "You know it, and he still pretends he doesn't have the hots for her."

"Your brother is weird. We all know that. If anyone is going to wear him down, it'll be Sophie."

"That we do. She's made it her life's mission to bring him to his knees." Emersyn smiles softly, staring off into space. "Brady."

"Yeah?" I respond, but she doesn't say anything. We stare at each other for a few minutes before the need to say something to fill the silence overcomes me. "The air filter on your car was clogged. It was an easy fix. I also changed your oil and all the filters just to be safe. If the light comes back on, we can hook it to my scan tool and find out what's going on."

"You didn't—" she begins, but I cut her off.

"I wanted to. I'd do anything to make sure you are safe, Em."

"Don't call me that," she chokes out, tears collecting in her eyes as she steps away from me and heads back toward the desk. "Thanks for fixing my car. You can leave the keys on the counter."

I grip her hand in mine, pulling her to a stop. "Talk to me, Em. I doubt your boyfriend would have a problem with us just talking."

Her entire body stiffens before she yanks her hand from my grasp. "What's on your mind, Em?"

This isn't how I wanted this conversation to go at all. I had planned on trying to figure out if she had a boyfriend and how they felt about each other before putting my plan into action, but things were getting uncomfortable quickly. We need to talk this out sooner rather than later, but I was honestly hoping for later.

"Why did you leave without a word?" Emersyn whispers, wrapping her arms around her waist as if to protect herself from my answer. "I know you had a war to fight, but you could've at least returned an email or a letter. I doubt they had you so busy over there that you couldn't send a simple note saying, *I'm not dead.*" She spins around to face me, her eyes blazing with a million emotions at once—anger, sadness, betrayal, hope, and love. "I poured my heart out to you that night, and you just left. You didn't even have the decency to tell me goodbye. You just vanished without a trace."

"Em." I reach out, wanting to pull her into my arms and tell her everything I've been feeling over the last year.

"No, Brady." She steps out of my reach. "You don't get to come home and make everything better with a smile and an apology."

"I *am* sorry, Em. So sorry." My voice breaks toward the end of my sentence, suddenly overcome with the realization that she may have truly moved on with someone else, as I'd hoped.

"I told you I loved you! I poured my heart out to you before you went off to war without the promise of return. And you said *nothing*." Angry tears stream down her face, but she swipes them away quickly. "What makes matters worse is you made me believe you cared. That you had been dreaming about our first kiss for as long as I had."

"I had. I still do." I step toward her, but she takes another step away from me. "It's the first thing I see when I close my eyes at night. I dream about how things would've turned out if Beckett hadn't walked outside when he did. How I'd have told you that I love you to the point of madness. That I can't breathe without you beside me. That I spent the entire time I was over there feeling as if a piece of my soul was missing because I left it here in Tyson's Creek with you."

"I...I can't, Brady." She hiccups as a sob escapes her

mouth, tears freely streaming down her cheeks. "I don't know if I can give you that part of me again."

"I understand, Em. I really do. I let your brother's words get into my head, convincing me that I'd never be good enough for you." I sigh, pulling her tightly into my chest, and her body stiffens. "And he was right: You do deserve better than me, but by some miracle, at some point, I was enough for you. Hopefully, I can be again."

Unable to resist, I brush my lips against hers, and an electric current shoots through my entire body like a live wire. I've been dreaming about her lips being pressed against mine since I walked out of my going away party, and my memories didn't do it justice. The feel of her body against mine, the smoothness of her skin as my calloused fingers caress her cheek, the sweet smile on her face...I want to remember this moment for the rest of my life. Imprint it on my heart as the first moment of our forever.

"Brady..."

"Don't say anything. I know there is someone in your life, but I can wait."

"Will you shut up for a second?" She snickers, placing her hand on my mouth. "I don't have a boyfriend." Her cheeks heat in embarrassment as she looks anywhere but into my eyes. "I said all those things to make you jealous and force you to respond to at least one of my emails."

I release a breath I didn't realize I was holding as I

rest my forehead against hers. "Thank fuck," I whisper before our lips come together again.

I pour all my feelings into this kiss, hoping she understands how much she means to me. We break apart, gasping for air, and I take a step back to put some much-needed space between us. "Now I don't have to feel bad about trying to win back your heart."

"What do you mean?"

"I mean, it's my turn to tell you how much I love you, Em. To show you with my actions, not just my words, how much you mean to me. You spent the last two years writing me emails and letters and sending care packages. Each one was proof of your commitment and love to me, even without an answer, and now it's my turn."

She stares at me for a few moments before a blinding smile spreads across her face and she responds, "Okay."

That's it. One simple, inconsequential word that means everything to me. "I should let you get back to work, but make sure to check your email, okay?"

"Sure," she responds as I back toward the entrance of the studio, not once taking my eyes off her. Somehow, I manage to make it out the door in one piece, with a goofy smile plastered on my face.

That worked out better than I could've ever imagined. It seems that convincing Emersyn we belong together is going to be easier than I thought.

ten

brady

It's been about a month since I told Emersyn how I felt in the waiting area of Barre Studio. I've taken my time responding to every email she sent while I was on deployment, but probably not in the way she expected. I don't pour my heart out to her or profess my undying love for her. Well, I do, but not in those words. Instead, I tell her about my day, the job site I'm working on, or random things that make me think of her. I want her to feel loved and cherished the way that she should've over the last two years. But I sign off every email telling her how much I love her and how I can't wait for us to spend the rest of our lives together.

But like how I acted during deployment, she hasn't responded to one email, which I should've expected. On top of that, we haven't been able to spend much time together either. Between her being a few hours' drive away at college during the week and the work over at the new construction site I'm working at, life has been busier than I'd like. I've sent her a few texts here and there, but she's only responded to a handful.

At first, I was nervous that she wasn't responding, my mind spiraling out of control with horrible scenarios of why she wasn't responding to me. However, Beckett put me out of my misery one night when I rushed into Crawdaddy's after work, begging him to tell me if she was okay. He said that finals were coming up, so she'd been studying.

"Hey Brady, you coming out for a drink tonight?" Ren, one of my coworkers, asks as he shoves his time-card into the slot to punch out for the weekend.

"Nah. I want to take advantage of the free Wi-Fi here in the office and send a few emails."

"You don't have Wi-Fi at home?"

"I do, but I also have a roommate at home," I respond, causing Ren to laugh loudly at my expense.

"Suit yourself. If you change your mind, we'll be at Crawdaddy's until Beckett kicks us out." He claps me on the back. "Maybe we can find you someone to spend time with besides that computer."

"I'm writing emails, jackass. Besides, I'm a one-woman kinda man."

"Ah, Emersyn Carter." He flashes me a knowing smirk. "Did you finally convince her to give you the time of day?"

Ren was there the first night I saw Emersyn after returning home and got an earful the minute she walked away from the table that she was off-limits. Even though, at the time, I thought she had a boyfriend, I knew that if she began dating someone on my crew, I'd bury the body and help everyone look for it.

Once Ren walks out the door, I check the break room for anyone else before turning around and taking a seat at one of the staff computers. I shake the mouse a few times to wake it up and then log in and pull up my email. It only took me a few minutes to find the next email from Emersyn for me to respond to.

Brady,

I can't begin to explain how much it bothers me you have such a boring email address. Like you couldn't come up with a special nickname or a play on words for your name? I mean get a little creative, will you! I think that's what I'm going to do for you when you come home: make you a fun email address. But it will be an email that we only use to message each other. I'll even make one for myself. Maybe I'd stop jumping out of my seat each time my email pings on my phone, only to be let down when the email isn't from you.

I know you haven't responded to any

of my emails or letters, but I can't stop writing to you. I constantly check my email, waiting to see if you've responded, even if it is just to tell me to fuck off, and my heart sinks each time I don't see one from you. Everyone thinks I'm being stupid. That ignoring me is your way of telling me you feel nothing for me, but that kiss wasn't my imagination.

I know Beckett must have said something to you that made you run away from me. I wish that he would stop treating me like a little girl. Yes, I understand he's my big brother and wants to protect me, but he doesn't need to worry about that with you. You two have been best friends for as long as I can remember, and you're one of the only non-family members I feel comfortable with. That should tell both of you something.

Love You Always,
Emersyn

I'm reading this email for what's probably the millionth time, but this time, something is different. No longer am I reading it for any information that would let me know Emersyn was moving on or that she no was longer willing to wait for me to come home. Instead, I can read it for what it was: her plea to know how I truly felt. I take a deep breath in and shake out my hands before I begin typing out my response to Emersyn.

Emersyn:

Baby, I'm so sorry. Honestly, I read this email a million times while I was deployed. I would search for even the smallest hint that you might have found someone else. Someone worthy of your love, but each time, I was relieved that you haven't.

I know that writing these emails to you now that I'm stateside probably isn't the same, but I wanted to give it a try. I wanted to make sure that you knew that even if I didn't write back to you, I read every single email. You can even ask Seth if you don't believe me. With each one I read, my resolve crumbled a little more each time. I love you with all my heart, and being away from you for any amount of time is almost unbearable, but I didn't want you to have to spend every day waiting by the phone for me to call. I wanted you to go to parties and live life to its fullest, but I guess you waited anyway. And for that, I'm grateful.

I never believed I deserved someone like you. Someone so honest, caring, and full of life. I kept my feelings for you locked up inside my heart because I let fear convince me that you wanted something else. That you wanted this grand life that I would never be able to give you. But after reading these letters again, I know there was only one thing you want from me: my heart.

But I can't give you what is already yours and always will be.

Love You Always,
Brady

After rereading the email and checking for any major spelling or grammatical errors, I hit send before shutting down the computer. I can't wait to see how she reacts to the surprise I have in store for her tomorrow. I just have to make a phone call first.

I make sure to lock up the office before pulling out

my phone and dialing the familiar number. Thankfully, he answers on the second ring.

"This better be important," Vance growls into the phone as I hear Selina groaning loudly.

"Why the fuck would you answer during sex?" My face wrinkles in disgust as Selina's laughter filters through the line

"We aren't having sex, asshole. I'm giving Selina a foot rub, and I need both hands. Oh, and you're on speakerphone."

"I gathered that much already." I chuckle softly as I unlock my truck and climb inside. "But it just so happens that I need to speak to your lady love more than you, anyway."

"Hey, Brady, what can I do for you?"

"Does Emersyn work tomorrow?" I ask, not wanting to waste any of her precious foot massage time.

"I believe so. Tomorrow is Tuesday, right?"

"Yup."

"Then yes, she does. Why?"

"Because I'm taking a dance class."

"You're doing what now?" Vance questions, his confusion clear in his voice.

"I'm going to take a dance class. I haven't been able to see her for almost a month because of our hectic work schedule and her studying for finals. I figure I can stumble my way through class and at least get five minutes with her."

"Awww, that's so stinking adorable," Selina coos into the phone. "Why didn't you ever do anything like that for me?"

"Because you pretended to hate me so I'd stay at arm's length." Vance chuckles.

"True." She giggles before speaking to me again. "Brady, the only class we have tomorrow is toddler ballet. It's a class of two- and three-year-olds. Do you think you can handle that?"

"I can do anything for her," I respond with conviction.

"Damn it, Brady. Tone it down. You're making all the rest of us men look bad."

"I'll try, but I make no promises." I chuckle softly as Selina tells me everything I need to know about attending the class.

I was hoping that the class she was teaching tomorrow was at least for teenagers, but I'll take what I can get. I want Emersyn to know I'd move heaven and earth to be with her, even if that means taking a ballet class with a bunch of toddlers.

eleven

brady

Sending emails to Emersyn has quickly become my favorite part of the day. I had originally planned on responding to emails once every few days, but once I started reading them, the floodgates opened. I wanted to know how different the emails would read now that I've pulled my head out of my ass. The guys give me a tough time about how excited I am to sit down and write emails, but I don't give a shit. Having this special time with Emersyn is important. I don't want her to have any doubt in her mind about what she means to me.

"Did you just send off another email, lover boy?" Jasper's southern drawl catches my attention as I walk into the break room.

My good mood immediately evaporates. "None of your business. I'm starting to regret not ensuring this place was empty before sending the last one."

"You say that almost every day, and do you honestly expect us not to say anything about it? Hell, some of us are jealous as fuck that we don't have someone like that in our lives," Easton pipes in from his seat next to Jasper.

Since I started working here, I've been spending the most time with these two, so I'm sure they can tell my mood swings better than the others. I know they are happy for me and aren't trying to give me a hard time about it, but something inside me feels as if I'm betraying whatever this is between us by sharing it with anyone but her.

"Can either of you do me a favor?" I ask, taking a seat on the other side of them.

"Depends. What do you want?" Jasper responds with a sinister smile on his face. "And what are you going to give me?"

Whatever he is up to can't be good, but I need their help if I'm going to pull off this next surprise for Emersyn. "You'll have my gratitude, and I'll owe you one, to be collected at the date of your choice."

"Sold. What do you need?" Easton chimes in, causing Jasper to scowl in his direction.

"I need someone to cover for me this afternoon. Vance already knows, but he said I needed to find someone to cover my shift at the new site."

"You're in luck. I had this afternoon off because I was going to pick up some hours on Saturday. I'll have to check with Connor about the schedule switch, but I don't anticipate it being an issue."

"Awesome. Thanks, man. All right, I'm headed to the back office to respond to some emails." I get up from my seat and head toward the door. "I'll be in the back office. Just let me know what he says."

"Will do." Easton gives me a mock salute as I turn and head toward the back of the building.

My skin itches with need as I inch closer to the office and take a seat at the empty computer. The anticipation of sitting down at the computer, wondering if Emersyn has had a chance to write back, bubbles under the surface as I wake up the monitor and log into my email.

Emersyn made it clear how much she loved me that day in her parents' backyard, and I said nothing. I can't even imagine how hurt she felt when I left without a word. Then I didn't respond to any emails she sent, but she kept sending them. She's a better human than I could ever be, and I'm going to spend the rest of my life making this up to her.

Is this how she felt every time her phone pinged with a notification of a new email, only to have her hopes dashed when she didn't have a response from me? If it is, I feel even worse for putting her through this. I know Emersyn is safe and sound, for the most part, as she goes to her classes and visits her friends, but she didn't have any of that same certainty about me. She had no idea if I was even alive with each passing day, and my radio silence more than likely made the pain even worse.

My shoulders sag as the computer comes to life, and I have no new emails. I figured she wouldn't have emailed me back, but a part of me hoped that after the email I sent last night, I'd get something, any hint that everything I've been sending her way is working. I have a lot—and I mean a *lot*—to make up for, but I can't give up hope that there's a chance for us, even if it isn't anytime soon.

"Stop moping, Brady. You got yourself into this mess, and now you need to man up and get yourself out of it," I say to myself, before searching my inbox and finding the exact email I'm looking for.

I remember the day I opened this email. It was the same day that I finally convinced Seth to move back to Tyson's Creek. He had been moping around, angry at himself and the world for not finding another way to get in contact with Bristol, but I laid it out for him. All he had to do was show her that he wanted to be with her. That she was the most important thing in his life. Not the Marines, but her. Apparently, I'm better at giving advice than I am at taking it because it took me until I was smacked in the face with the reality that Emersyn may have moved on and given up on us that I took action.

BRADY MICHAEL THOMAS, I

COULD STRANGLE YOU RIGHT NOW! You and my brother have lost your minds if you think that you have any say on what I do and don't do with my life.

When I kissed you that night, I did it because I wanted to. Because I have loved you for years but couldn't come up with the courage to tell you. I was afraid that things would become weird between us or that you'd pull away from me completely. So, I kept it all bottled up inside, locked away from everyone but Sophie. But I kept telling myself that having you in my life in any way was better than not at all, and for a while, that was okay. But it killed me inside. I kept wondering what I'd do if you showed up one night with a girlfriend and how I would react. Would I be able to keep it together? Would I be able to see you happy with someone else? And I knew that I couldn't, so I worked up the courage to tell you. And then you disappeared without a word.

I smacked Beckett when he told me what he said to you. I'm the only person *who can determine who is and who isn't worthy of my love. And I chose you. And what did you do? You ran away from me. You're an asshole, Brady! Do you know that? You could have done or said anything to me, and I'd have been fine. You should have told me the bullshit Beckett was spewing, but instead, you ran. Why? Why have you not said a word to me since that night? It's been months without a word. Is that your answer? For some reason, I can't bring myself to believe that, so I'll keep writing to you, hoping that my words reach you, and you'll finally understand how much you mean to me.*

Love You Always,
Emersyn

The first time I read this email, I didn't know what to say to her. How to apologize for the pain Beckett and I put her through. I thought I needed to find the perfect way to explain what happened, but in reality, all I needed to do was be honest with her. That's all she's ever wanted from me, and it's about time I start giving it to her because she needs to know. It's the only way we'll be able to find our way back to each other.

Emersyn,

You're right. I'm an asshole. I knew that at the time, and I know that now. But that doesn't change anything. I know I should apologize for everything that has happened since that night in your parents' backyard, but my words aren't enough this time. This is why I've been writing you these emails. Well, that, and it's easier for me to write out my feelings than try and tell you. Based on this email, I have a feeling you'd smack me or, even worse, punch me in the nose for what I'm about to say.

I believed Beckett. Every word he said that night was the same thing I'd been thinking since I realized how I felt about you. I tried to hide how I felt from your brother, but I know he noticed the way I would look at you sometimes or how I couldn't help but follow behind you like a lost puppy whenever you were in the same room with us. You became my sun, and I gravitated around you whenever I could. I wanted to be wherever you were, even at the cost of spending time with him or my family. I'm sure he noticed. I can't help but wonder if this was why he became so overprotective of you.

I tried to hide my feelings for you, but Beckett isn't stupid. One night when I was home on leave, he told me that I needed to stay away from you for your own good because I wasn't good enough for you. Deep down, I knew that. I knew you deserved someone better than me who could give you a stable life and everything you could ever want in life. But after that moment, those feelings began to consume me. Each time he noticed me staring too long or paying a little too much attention to you, he'd remind me that I wasn't good enough for his sister. But I was determined to be better for you. I was a Marine, serving my country, but I couldn't give you any promises that I would come home. I couldn't keep you safe and give you the reassurance of knowing I was going to be coming home to you every day. And those things only made Beckett double down even more. Now, not only was I not good enough, but I also was going to die and leave you heartbroken, and that's what hit me the most.

If I'm being honest, that's why I left that night. I knew there was no guarantee I would make it home from deployment. That you'd spend the rest of your life mourning what we could've been instead of living life to the fullest. And for that, I'm sorry. I did the one thing I never wanted to do. I took away your choice.

You're right. Neither I nor Beckett has the right to make decisions for you. I can't speak for him, but I'll try never to do it again. I say try because I know I'll fuck up and need to ask for your forgiveness again. I'm human, after all, but I promise you that I'll try. But I can promise I'm never leaving you or Tyson's Creek again. I will love you until my heart stops beating, even if you can't find it in your heart to forgive me. I promise to always be there for you, to listen to what you have to say, and to always put your happiness above everything else.

So, here is the answer you've been looking for all these years. I love you,

Emersyn Grace Carter. The all-consuming, forever kind of love, and I'll spend the rest of my life proving it to you.

Love You Always,
Brady

twelve

emersyn

"How the hell am I supposed to keep my heart locked away from that?" I huff, flopping back on the bed beside Sophie.

I've read every email Brady has sent in response to the ones I sent while he was deployed. Some of them are exactly what I'd have expected him to say, telling me small things about his day and what he's up to or that he misses me, but suddenly, they become more personal. It's as if he's pouring his heart out to me in the lines of these emails, wanting me to know the man he is now rather than the one who left me without a word two years ago. Sophie and the girls keep asking me if I'm ready to give him another chance at my heart, but I still don't know the answer.

I want to open up more to Brady and give him a chance to get to know the person I am now, but there's also a part of me that's afraid to open up to him again. He's retired from the military and home in Tyson's

Creek for good, but what happens if he changes his mind again? Or if Beckett suddenly has issues with us being together again? I don't know if I'll be able to survive that level of heartache.

"You don't." Sophie lays her head on my shoulder, bringing my mind back to the present. "He told you he was on a mission to prove to you how much he cares about you, and this is his way of doing it."

"But these are just pretty words on paper." Tears pool in my eyes as I try to process everything he said in this last message.

"Do you honestly believe Brady would do that to you again? Or, better yet, that Beckett would want to hurt you like that again?"

Things were strained between my brother and me after he told me about his and Brady's conversation. I was so angry at him for chasing Brady away, but I was more hurt that both still saw me as someone so weak. That I was too naïve and couldn't understand the gravity of my own feelings. I know in my heart that both were trying to protect me from the pain of losing Brady if something had happened, but it wasn't either of their choices to make.

The day after Brady fixed my car and told me his plan to win my heart a second time, I went to see my brother. I wanted to make sure that Beckett knew not to interfere this time. He promised to try his best to keep out of it, but all bets were off if Brady hurt me again, and I can't blame him. Beckett might be his best friend, but my happiness will always come first.

"Do you believe him?" Sophie asks, rolling to her side and resting her cheek on her hand.

"Who?" I know damn well who she's speaking about, but I don't want to answer.

There's no doubt in my mind that Brady Thomas is in love with me. I knew it deep in my bones when he kissed me that night, but I'm not sure if I can trust it. I know it seems crazy; if I were to ask anyone, they'd say the same thing, even without knowing what happened over the last two years. And little by little, the walls around my heart are crumbling down. I just hope I'm not opening myself up for heartbreak a second time.

"Don't play dumb, Em."

"Yes. I believe him, but I'm afraid he's going to change his mind. If he did, I don't think I would survive it."

"You would because you're the strongest person I know, but I don't think you'll have to. Just give it some more time. I know deep down everything will work out the way that it should."

I sit up on the bed and wrap my arms around Sophie's waist, allowing the tears to flow freely down my cheeks. These aren't tears of sadness but tears full of so many emotions that I need to let them free. I can't continue to keep my feelings for him bottled up inside, or I'm going to explode. Brady has spent the last month filling in the missing pieces and helping me understand his reasoning behind not responding to my emails. Now my heart just needs him to prove it.

thirteen

brady

"Did you seriously all have to come?" I grumble as I walk in through the front door of Barre Studio with Vance, Walker, Riggs, and Connor in tow. Vance rushes in, making a beeline for his wife, Selina.

Selina's entire face lights up with a brilliant smile as she notices Vance headed her way. Her lightly tanned skin is accentuated by her chocolate brown hair, which is pulled back in a tight bun at the nape of her neck, the typical hairstyle for a ballerina. It's in drastic contrast to how I've seen her outside of the studio, hair hanging loosely down her back. Selina is slightly taller than I remember, standing only a few inches shorter than Vance. I watch as Vance leans down and plants a kiss on her small baby bump. Her hands thread through his hair before tugging it lightly to get his attention.

I know I should stop watching them, but my heart yearns for that future. One where Emersyn looks at me like I hung the moon as I murmur to our little one about how much I love them and can't wait to meet them. I want all of that and so much more, and it's within my grasp. If I can convince Emersyn to give me a chance.

I've told her I'm going to show her how much she means to me, and the emails are a great start, but I still have a long way to go. I originally came up with the plan to come to the dance studio as a way to see Emersyn without disrupting her schedule, but after seeing those two together, I want more. I want to take her out on a date, to hold her hand, to let everyone know that we have finally found our way back to each other. But is she ready?

"I'll catch up with you guys in a few minutes." Connor's voice brings me back to the present as he claps me on the shoulder and heads toward a group of teenagers standing on the other side of the room.

I watch as two of the teenagers smile brightly in his direction before taking turns wrapping him up in a tight hug. I must have some sort of look on my face because Walker answers my unspoken question. "The one on the right is his daughter, Jade. The other, slightly shorter girl is his stepdaughter, Love. She's Audrey's daughter. Audrey is Selina, Bristol, and Leia's other bestie who moved here a few years ago."

Well, that makes a little more sense now that he's explained it. I vaguely remember Seth saying something about Bristol's best friend moving to help her at Nurture Space, her yoga studio. However, I wasn't really paying attention to all the details. I've been a little preoccupied with my own love life at the moment.

"Okay, Connor and Vance tagging along makes sense. Connor came so he could surprise his daughters, and Vance's wife owns this place, but why you two?"

"Do you honestly think we'd miss seeing you trying to do some intricate dance moves? I think not." Riggs chuckles, wrapping his arm around my shoulder.

Riggs and Walker have been spending more and more time here in town over the last few weeks as Mr. Armstrong's health continues to decline. I've been to visit them a few times, and it's obvious that there's something more wrong with him than his heart, but he keeps telling Walker and his sisters not to worry about it. Which basically means they are going to worry even more.

"I needed the distraction," Walker grumbles as he files into the studio behind me. "And a break from my dad. I love him, but he really needs to accept I don't want to take over Tranquility Retreat."

"He still won't give it a rest?" I question as my head swivels from side to side, searching for Emersyn.

"No. He's even started asking Leia to run things by me before making purchases and stuff."

"Oh, I doubt that's going over well." I chuckle as I continue scanning the room, searching for my girl.

"Leia isn't having it and has basically told Walker to fuck off more than once in the last week." Riggs holds the door open for a mom and her little girl before heading further into the waiting room. "You know, if she got married, he wouldn't give her a hard time anymore. He could pass the business down to her and her husband. Easy solution."

"Trying to take over your family business *is not* a good reason to marry someone." Walker cuffs him on the back of the head. "Although maybe you'll man up and ask her and solve both of your problems."

"You and Leia? Get Married?" I snort loudly but stop when I notice the serious look on his face. "I thought you were joking."

"No. It's not a joke. I'd ask her right this second if I knew she'd say yes, but she hates my guts."

"And whose fault is that? If you would stop trying to push her buttons like a child on the playground, things would run a lot smoother," Walker says, daring him to tell him he's wrong.

I always knew there was a story behind the love-hate relationship that Leia and Riggs have with each other, but never knew what it was.

"We aren't talking about this right now," he grumbles before dropping into an empty seat against the wall between two women around our age.

"Take it from someone who is regretting every choice he's made over the last two years and some change: Don't wait to make things right with the woman you love, or you'll lose her," I respond as he turns his back to me, focusing all his attention on the mother beside him and her daughter.

"Hello, little lady. Are you here for the dance class today?" Riggs wiggles his fingers toward her, but she grasps onto his fingers tightly, pulling him forward and almost out of the chair.

"Yes! I wuv Ms. E's 'ass," she responds with a toothy grin as we all stifle a laugh.

Her mom's cheeks pink slightly as her eyes scan down Riggs's body before snapping back to his. "Do you have a daughter taking class today?"

"Oh, gods, no," he chokes out but quickly catches himself. "I haven't been lucky enough to find the right woman to have children with. I'm here to help this guy convince a girl to go on a date with him." He motions over his shoulder in my direction, and I force a smile onto my face.

The two women eye me skeptically before saying a hasty goodbye to Riggs, wrapping their children in their arms, and heading toward the other side of the waiting area. As soon as they reach the other side of the room where the other mothers are, they begin whispering softly to them, glancing every so often in our direction, and I can't blame them. I'm a grown man in his mid-thirties, hanging out at a dance studio with my two very single friends, talking about finding someone to go on a date with.

"You could've tried harder to explain things to

them," I grumble, the anxiety from earlier returning at full force. Every possible way that things could go wrong with me showing up here filters through my mind. What if she doesn't show up for work today? Does she not want to see me? I've asked Selina not to say anything to her because I want it to be a surprise, but Selina and I aren't friends. Emersyn has been working here for over two years at this point, and Selina trusts her.

"Stop panicking," Walker says, gripping my shoulder tightly to ground me.

"I'm not panicking," I choke out. My eyes scan the entire waiting area, looking for some sign of Emersyn, and come up empty.

"Yes, you are. It's written all over your face," Riggs responds from my other side as I ease into the chair beside him and drop my head into my hands. "The worst thing that can happen is that she doesn't want to go on a date with you."

"No, the worst thing that could happen is she never speaks to me again, and I have to watch her run off into the sunset with some douchebag that isn't good enough for her."

"Fair point." They both chuckle softly as Walker takes the now-empty seat on the other side of Riggs. "But do you really believe that's what's going to happen?"

I take a deep breath, trying to calm my nerves so I

can think clearly. If Emersyn hated me that much, she never would've let me get closer to her the day I dropped off her car. She wouldn't have kissed me. She damn sure wouldn't have told me she lied about having a boyfriend either. She loves me. I know it deep in my soul, so why would she refuse to at least have dinner with me?

"No." My entire body sags in the seat as the tension leaves my body. "But I don't know if coming here for a toddler dance class was the best idea."

"Maybe not, but nothing proves that you're head over heels for a girl than being willing to make an ass of yourself," Connor says as he comes to a stop in front of us, his two daughters standing on either side of him with their arms threaded through his.

"And who might these beauties be?" Riggs runs his hand through his wavy hair and winks in their direction. "I didn't know you had any sisters."

"You must be Riggs. Auntie Leia has told us all about you," one of the girls responds, her eyes scanning him in judgment.

I have a feeling that's Audrey's daughter, Love. I've only seen her a handful of times around town, but there are enough pictures sitting on Connor's desk of him and his girls to be able to tell who is who. Besides, she looks almost exactly like her mother. Love's dark-colored hair is piled on the top of her head in an almost perfect bun, a few stray curls hanging out the front, framing her face. Her long legs are wearing the usual pale pink tights, but instead of the sheer pink skirt and black leotard I'm used to seeing Emersyn wear, she has on a pair of light blue cutoff jean shorts, a Nirvana T-shirt, and a pair of bright purple Converse high-tops covering her feet.

"Good things, I hope..." He winks at the other girl, who is most likely Jade, but she flashes him a dirty look, as well.

"No," Jade responds, causing the rest of us to burst out into loud, boisterous laughter before turning her attention toward me. "And you're Brady."

Jade has the same dark-colored hair as Love, pulled into a messy bun on the top of her head, a few stray curls hanging out the back, brushing the shoulders of the green oversized shirt hanging off her shoulder, exposing the black leotard underneath. Her long legs are encased in a pair of black yoga pants and a pair of black Converse sneakers.

"Yes?" I respond with a questioning tone, not wanting to be on this side of her judgmental stare. If looks could kill, I would be dead right now. If I wasn't so terrified for our safety at the moment, I'd feel sorry for Connor. I never want to be on the other end of their disapproving gazes again.

"Good," is her only response before she pulls her phone out of her pocket, and her fingers begin to fly across the screen. After a few moments, she shoves her phone back into her pocket and smiles brightly at me.

"Why good?" Walker asks.

"You'll see," Love responds with the same Cheshire cat smile on her face as she wiggles her phone in front of my face.

This. Can. Not. Be. Good. I open my mouth to ask her what she means when the door swings open beside me.

Leia, Bristol, and Audrey come spilling into the studio. Their heads move on a swivel, searching for something before locking on our small group. All three of them move as one, making a beeline in our direction.

"Why didn't you tell me this is where you were going?" Leia asks as she comes to a stop right in front of her brother.

Leia's blonde hair is pulled into a ponytail near the top of her head; a few tendrils of hair have escaped and are framing her face. She's dressed casually in a pair of black yoga pants and an oversized sweatshirt hanging slightly off her right shoulder. Her wire-frame glasses are perched on the end of her nose, and thick black eyelashes frame her crystal blue eyes, which are locked on Walker.

"Because you weren't invited." Walker smirks up at her before leaning back and crossing his arms over his chest.

"Neither were you. None of you were," I murmur,

not wanting to draw any more attention to our group that we already have.

"Shh... no one asked you." Leia wiggles her finger in my direction, her eyes never leaving Walker's face. "Hell, you brought him"—nodding toward Riggs—"and not your own sister? I'm hurt."

"Don't feel slighted, darlin'. I invited you. Isn't that enough?" Riggs responds, his southern drawl out in full force as he reaches for Leia's hand, brushing his lips against it.

Leia's cheeks pink slightly, her entire body melting at his words. For a few moments, she looks like she is in pure heaven, but then her face morphs into what looks like indifference before she pulls her hand free from his grasp, putting some space between them.

"Sending me a text that says *I miss you. Come to Barre in* 30, isn't inviting me anywhere. It's the quickest way to make me want to *not* go somewhere."

"Really? Is that why you changed your clothes almost twenty times before we could leave your place to meet the girls for lunch?" Bristol bumps her friend's shoulder, causing her cheeks to turn pink in embarrassment.

This is the first time I've seen Bristol since we came home from deployment. I keep asking Seth to bring her by, but he seems to want to keep whatever is going on between the two of them to himself, and I can't blame him. It's one of the reasons why I haven't said anything to him about what's going on between Emersyn and me, as well.

Bristol's red hair lays over her shoulder in an intricate braid, with a few stray tendrils of hair framing her face. Her entire body is still completely toned from teaching yoga for a living and is encased in her usual attire of yoga pants and a fitted top. A smile tugs at the corner of her mouth as she leans down and plants a kiss on my cheek.

"Not with Seth today?" I ask, giving her a short hug.

"No. He had to work. I assume that's your fault since you're here and he isn't?"

"No. That had nothing to do with me." I raise my hands in surrender before pointing to Connor and Audrey, standing off to the side of the group. "Blame Connor. He owns the place and makes the schedule:"

"I would, but my bestie might be a little angry at me if I did." Bristol giggles, but my eyes remain focused on Audrey and Connor.

Jade and Love are standing off to the side, speaking in hushed tones with some of their friends, but I can't stop the pang of jealousy I feel as Connor wraps his arms around Audrey and pulls her into his side. I could have had this with Emersyn if I'd pulled my head out of my ass sooner.

"Not my fault. Blame Vance." Connor snickers as

he leans down and plants a kiss on the top of Audrey's hair.

"What's my fault?" Vance asks, as if appearing out of thin air. His fingers thread through Selina's as they come to a stop on the left side of Walker. "I see the gang is all here to witness our boy make a fool of himself."

"Almost everyone. Apparently, I get to blame you for Seth still being at work and not being able to make our lunch date."

"Guilty as charged, but someone had to work so the rest of us could be here to watch the show."

"Or you could all leave," I grumble, leaning back in the chair and crossing my arms.

"What would be the fun in that?" Selina giggles softly. "But I work here. And I made sure all the moms stopped looking at you like a lunatic ready to pounce on the first beautiful woman you saw."

"And that's my fault," Riggs chuckles.

"Why does this not surprise me?" Leia responds just as the bell chimes above the door.

I turn toward the sound of the noise and notice Emersyn walk into the studio, and I freeze. My eyes scan her body, taking in the fitted grey top covering her curvy frame and the way her apple bottom fills out a pair of black yoga pants. Images of sinking my teeth into that ass as I take her from behind fill my mind, creating a rising problem in my pants.

"What are all of you doing here?" Emersyn's eyes widen in surprise as I push to my feet and head toward her.

"I missed you," I whisper, wrapping my arms around her waist and pulling her tightly to me. Her hands make their way around my shoulders, and she tugs on my neck, pulling me toward her. Our lips connect, and I pour all my feelings into this one kiss, hoping I convey my love to her without using words.

"It seems as if she missed you a little, too," someone says from behind me, and she ducks her head into my chest.

I plant a kiss on the top of her head before leaning down to whisper into her ear. "I know I promised to give you space, but I needed to see you. You've been busy studying for finals, so I figured if I took one of your classes, I could get my fix and be okay for a while."

"Huh?" She pulls away from me, her eyes searching my face for something.

"I needed an Emersyn recharge." I swipe my thumb across her cheek, her skin feeling like silk beneath my calloused fingers.

I can't take it anymore; I need to ask her. I don't care that we're standing in front of a room full of our friends, and even some strangers. I had this grand plan to show her how much she means to me, and I can still do that, but I need to spend more time with her. I need it like I need my next breath, and judging by the look in her eye, she wants that, too.

I open my mouth to ask her, but she beats me to it. "Have dinner with me," she blurts out. It's a statement, not a request. It seems she's just as anxious for us to spend some time together as I am.

"Sure." I smile before all our friends groan loudly in disappointment.

"Aww, man. I was really looking forward to watching Brady make a fool of himself," Riggs complains, pushing to his feet and grabbing Leia's hand. "But now I can go have lunch with this beautiful lady instead. That's a win in my book."

"I'm not going anywhere with you," she responds, trying to pull her hand free from his grasp.

"How about we all go have lunch together since we're here? Emersyn has a class to teach, but the rest of us can head to the diner," Audrey recommends, as she's obviously the only one able to read the room. Riggs nods his head before tightening his grasp on Leia's hand and pulling her out the door.

"Heck, yeah. I've been craving a chicken sandwich with pickles." Selina rubs her hand across her baby bump and licks her lips.

"What my lady wants, my lady gets," Vance responds, placing a kiss on the side of her head and pulling her out the door, with Connor and Audrey hot on their heels.

"Thank fuck. I thought they'd never leave," I whisper, running my nose along the shell of her ear.

"I mean, you brought them with you." She giggles softly, her eyes shining with happiness.

"No, I didn't. They all just kind of appeared."

"So, nothing out of the ordinary." She smiles, brushing her lips across mine and stepping out of my embrace. "Dinner?"

"Tonight, at my place."

"I'll text you when I'm on my way over," she says softly as I begin backing toward the door, not wanting to take my eyes off her for a second.

"I can't wait," I respond, bumping into the door and pitching forward.

Emersyn giggles softly as I stumble, barely stopping myself from falling flat on my face. I stand up quickly. My cheeks heat as I give her an awkward wave and head out the door.

Any other day, I'd be beyond embarrassed. I'm a thirty-eight-year-old man, acting like a complete idiot in front of the girl he loves, but none of that matters. Because I have a date with my girl.

fourteen

brady

Instead of heading to the diner to meet my friends, I go right home, shooting off a text to Seth on the way to tell him to find someone's couch to sleep on tonight. He's just put in an offer on a house a few days ago, so hopefully, this will be the one and only time I have to kick him out to spend time alone with Emersyn. With Seth and Bristol getting closer, I'm sure he's itching to be able to have a place of his own, as well. I mentioned something about him just moving in with her, but he shot that idea down immediately. He doesn't want to put pressure on Bristol to define their relationship. He's happy to move at her pace, however fast or slow that might be, but he also needs a space of his own. I know he barely knows anyone in town—hell, he could probably ask to sleep in my old room at my mom's place—but he owes me. It's my turn to woo my girl.

As soon as I pull my truck into the driveway, I bolt

up the stairs. The moment I'm through the door, I scan the apartment, looking for anything out of place. Thankfully, Seth is a clean freak, so there doesn't seem to be much out of place. Our apartment is small, but there's more than enough space for two bachelors. We have a decent-sized living room, with a small sectional pushed up against the outer wall and a sixty-inch TV mounted on the wall across from it, separating the living room from the kitchen. There's a small table in the kitchen, enough space for Seth and me to eat, although we usually eat on the sofa if we even eat up here.

Once I grab the few items out of place and put them away, I head into the only bathroom and turn on the shower. I've been working most of the morning and didn't have time to shower before leaving work and heading to the dance studio. I figured I'd work up a sweat there anyway, so it didn't matter. But now, I think a shower is in order.

Before hopping into the shower, I head across the hall to my bedroom and curse softly under my breath. This place is a fucking mess. There's dirty laundry spread all over the floor and a few half-empty cups and beer cans sitting on the table beside my bed. Seth is the clean one in our friendship, hence the clean common area.

"This place is gross," I murmur, my shower completely forgotten.

Since I'm already here, I get to work, grabbing everything splayed on the floor and quickly making my bed. I'm not naïve enough to think Emersyn and I won't end up in here at some point, but that's not my intention.

I'm taking things slow with her, wanting to ensure she knows what's happening between us is the real thing. That she doesn't have to be afraid. But I understand if she's hesitant around me. I'm the man who broke her heart, but I'm asking for her forgiveness and another chance. It's a lot easier to forgive, but asking for another chance may be too much.

Shoving all the laundry into the hamper, I decide to take it one step further and head back into the kitchen. It takes me a few minutes, but I find the rest of the cleaning supplies and head back into my room to dust every surface I can think of until it sparkles.

"Much better," I say into the now-spotless room before grabbing some clean boxers out of my dresser and heading back across the hall to the bathroom.

The small bathroom is completely full of steam from leaving the water running for so long, but I immediately shuck off my clothes and climb into the water. "Fuck. That's hot!" I yell, jumping back out of the shower, reaching for the knob, and turning it down. I wait a few seconds, making sure to check the water temperature this time, before stepping back in.

I make quick work of washing, taking extra time to

wash the sawdust and dirt from my hair before turning the water off and towel-drying myself. Once I'm in my clear pair of boxers, I bend down and clean up the water off the floor, hang my towel on the hook behind the door, and stride back into my bedroom.

Just as I'm entering the room, my phone pings with the sound of an incoming text. Diving across the bed, I snatch my phone off the end table where I left it and read a text from Emersyn.

EM

On my way.

FUCK! How long did it take for me to clean my room and take a shower? I assumed I'd have a few hours before Emersyn arrived, but I guess she was as anxious for us to spend time together as I was.

BRADY

See you soon. xoxo

I add on a few kisses and hugs for good measure before dropping my phone onto the bed and grabbing the first pair of clean jeans and shirt I can put my hands on. I dress quickly and head into the bathroom to tame my hair. The just-got-out-of-bed look that women love is anything but easy to recreate. It takes a lot of product and some carefully placed hairs to get a look that seems effortless. But I don't have enough time for that, so I take a glob of pomade, warm it up in my hands, and run it through my hair, sending up a silent prayer that it behaves.

After one final glance in the mirror, the doorbell rings, signaling her arrival. I rush toward the front door, stopping short to take a deep breath before opening the door. My breath catches in my throat as my eyes scan her body. Instead of the tight ballerina bun that I saw her with earlier today, her hair hangs loosely around her shoulders. She's wearing a black fitted top tucked into a pair of jeans shorts to torture me.

"I stopped at Sophie's house to shower and change after class. I hope that's okay," she says, her hand motioning between us. "We match."

I look down and notice I'm also wearing a black shirt tucked into a pair of dark-wash jeans and chuckle softly. "Great minds and all, right?" I open the door further and step to the side so she can come in.

"Right." Emersyn's eyes scan the room.

Although she'd been here before I left for deployment, I didn't have a roommate then. If she knew anything about Seth, she'd know that he travels light. Almost everything he owns fits into our military-issued duffel bags.

"Nothing much has changed. Just the spare bedroom is Seth's, and my video game equipment has been moved to the living room."

"Oh, what are you ever going to do?" She snickers before leaning against the now-closed door. "So, what are we having for dinner?"

I freeze, my eyes widening in surprise as I realize my mistake. I was so focused on making sure the place was presentable, I completely forgot about the food. Who the hell asks a date to come over for dinner and doesn't have dinner to feed said date? Not to mention I have no idea how to cook.

"You forgot I was coming, didn't you?" Emersyn says humorously, as she spins around and reaches for the door. "It's okay. We can do this another time."

I reach forward, grabbing her arm and spinning her around to face me. "You're so wrong, Emersyn. You have no idea how long I've wanted to tell you how much you mean to me."

I keep my grip on her arm, afraid that she might take off further into the house, before slamming the door shut.

"I wanted to make everything perfect before you came over, and I didn't even think about food." I sigh, pulling her tightly into my chest, and her body stiffens. "I wanted tonight to be perfect so I can tell you how much I love you. I tried before, but someone always interrupted us. But tonight is my chance to make sure you never doubt my feelings for you."

"But why? Why did you stop talking to me?" She pulls back, tilting her head up to look at me.

"I thought if I stopped contacting you, made a clean break, you'd forget about me."

Unable to resist, I brush my lips against hers, and an electric current shoots through my entire body like a live wire. I've been dreaming about her lips being pressed against mine for the last year, and my memories didn't do it justice. The feel of her body against mine, the smoothness of her skin as my calloused fingers caress her cheek, the sweet smile on her face...I want to remember this moment for the rest of my life. Imprint it on my heart as the first moment of our forever.

"I was an idiot who knew deep down I didn't deserve you. But I'm tired of trying to stay away from you," I whisper before our lips come together again. I pour all my feelings into this kiss, hoping she understands how much she means to me. We break apart, gasping for air, as I lift her into my arms. "You're the only person I want to be with, Emersyn. You're the air I breathe. My reason for living." I nip at the sensitive skin behind her ear. "Even when we were apart, all I could think about was getting home to you so we could start our lives together. Please tell me I'm not too late."

I spin around, pinning her to the door with my body. I know I should have made some grand gesture, showing her how loved and cherished she is, but I can't wait for her any longer. I'm unable to find the words to describe my feelings for her, but I can show her exactly how much I love her with my body.

She wraps her legs around my waist. "I love you, Brady."

I growl as I grind my cock into her pussy. "Say it again." I start nibbling down her neck and across her exposed collarbone.

"I love you." Emersyn moans, grinding her core down on me as I thrust forward, our need for each other building.

"I know I should take things slow, but I need you, Em. I've done nothing but dream about this moment since I watched you walk away from me and into that house the night before I left for deployment."

She wraps her arms around my neck before crushing her lips to mine, pulling me tightly to her. "Please make me yours."

I slide my hand between our bodies, shoving it down her pants and slipping a finger between her folds. She gasps in surprise, her head dropping back and hitting the door with a thump. Her juices drip down my hand as her walls tighten.

"You're so tight." I groan into her neck as I scissor my fingers, stretching her. "I can't wait to sink my cock deep inside you."

Emersyn moans, using her arms to lift her body and slide up and down my fingers. My thumb rubs slow, languid circles on her hardened nub.

"You want that, don't you? You want me to fuck you against this door like a dirty little girl?"

The filthy words tumble out of my mouth, and I'm unable to control them. Years of need for her have been building up to this moment, and I don't have the will to stop it. Emersyn will be mine before the end of the night. Now the only problem is deserving her. Her hips continue to rise and fall in time with my movements as she unwraps her arm from around my neck, reaching for the button of my jeans.

"I need you," she pants.

I pull my fingers from between her folds and shove them deep into my mouth. Her eyes widen as I lick them clean before lowering her feet to the floor.

"Turn around," I command as I flick the button of my jeans open and reach inside, fisting my cock tightly as I pull it out. I pump my fist up and down a few times, collecting the pre-cum leaking from the tip. Emersyn watches me, licking her lips in anticipation.

"Later, sweetheart. I'm barely holding on by a thread as it is. If I let you wrap your lips around my cock, I'll blow my load in a matter of seconds."

"That's a promise." She gives me a wink before slowly turning around, resting her hands on the door, and sticking her ass out into the air.

I shove her shorts and panties down to the floor and help her step out of them, throwing them over my shoulder. I massage each cheek in the palm of my hands as I rub my cock between them, bumping her puckered entrance. Emersyn raises onto her toes before pushing back once again.

"I plan to take you here. To own every part of your body." I lean forward, coating my length in her juices as I pull her earlobe between my teeth.

"Yes," she hisses, pushing back and taking me further into her core.

"I'm yours, Emersyn," I whisper into her ear before pulling back and slamming into her.

"Ouch," she whimpers.

My eyes widen in shock as the realization of what I've just done settles. She was a virgin, saving herself for the only man she has ever loved. And here I am, treating her like an animal ready to be bred instead of treating her like the angel she is.

"Why didn't you tell me?" I gasp.

I want nothing more than to rut myself deeper inside her pussy, claiming her as mine. The possessive need to mark her so no man will have a doubt about who she belongs to is overwhelming. But I won't hurt her any more than I already have.

"Because I knew you would make an excuse not to do it. I've waited all these years to be yours, Brady. Now finish what you started." Emersyn groans over her shoulder as she pushes her arms straight, shoving my cock deeper inside her. "I wouldn't have it any other way."

My loud groan fills the room as I grip her hips tightly, pulling her ass toward me as I thrust forward.

"Oh, yes. Right there. Don't stop," she begs.

I continue a slow pace, not wanting to hurt her, as I lick up her spine, latching on to her shoulder with my teeth.

"You were made for me." I groan as I pick up the pace, slamming into her.

The sound of our skin slapping against each other fills the room as I reach around, rolling both her nipples between my fingers. An inhuman sound leaves her lips as my cock slips out of her, and I step back. She looks over her shoulder, eyes hooded with desire, ready to do anything I command just to find her release.

"Spread your pussy lips for me. I want to see what's mine."

Emersyn does as I ask, reaching back and spreading her lips with her fingers. Her pink flesh is calling me as I fist my cock, pumping up and down slowly. Her eyes widen, and she licks her lips.

"Please," she begs.

But before she gets my cock again, I want to prolong our time together. Bring her more pleasure than she could ever imagine.

"Finger yourself. I'm going to fuck you hard and fast once I get back inside you, and I don't know how long I'll last. I want you to be ready for me."

Emersyn slowly plunges two fingers deep into her core before pulling them out slowly.

"Faster." I pump my cock in time with her movements, my balls pulling up and signaling my need for release.

I take a step forward, pulling her fingers from her pussy. I suck them deep into my mouth, licking them clean before gripping a handful of her hair and pulling her head back. Her back arches, and her round ass pushes against me.

"Everything that you are is mine, Emersyn. Do you understand? Now that I've had you, I'm never letting you go."

"Yes," she hisses.

I plunge my tongue back into her mouth as I slam back into her pussy, and her walls instantly construct around me.

"Do. Not. Fucking. Come," I say between clenched teeth as I flatten her body against the door, pounding into her with abandon. I know I should be gentle, but the need to possess her is almost unbearable.

"Scream for me, Em. I want everyone to know what we're doing. That you belong to me and no one else," I rasp.

There is nothing else but the two of us in this moment, our bodies coming together and making us one, bound in a way most people never feel.

"Come for me, baby," I whisper in her ear before pulling it between my lips and biting down hard.

Emersyn screams my name as her pussy clamps around me, milking my cock as she finds her release.

Blinding lights flash before my eyes as my knees buckle. I lean forward, resting my hand against the door for support as my breathing evens out, and I come back down to reality.

The weight of what I've done rests on my shoulders like an anvil, and my chest tightens. Beckett's words filter through my mind, reminding me once again that I never deserved Emersyn or the precious gift she just gave me. With a hiss, I pull out of her, bend down, and quickly pull up my pants.

"Everything they tell you in school about your first time is a lie." Emersyn smiles sweetly as she turns around, wrapping her arms around my neck once again and snuggling into my chest.

I wince as if she's smacked me across the face, her words cutting me right to the core.

Warring emotions fill my mind at the mention of the precious gift Emersyn has given me. Her first time should have been something to remember. Not a quick fuck against the door of my apartment.

"What's wrong, Brady?" She looks up at me, her eyes shining with love and adoration that I don't deserve.

"I have to go," I murmur, stepping out of her embrace.

Kissing her on the cheek, I rush out the door and head directly to my car on autopilot. The only thing on my mind is finding some way to make this up to her and show her how much she means to me, that she deserves so much more than what I just gave her.

It isn't until I'm sitting in front of the diner that I realize what a colossal mistake I've just made.

fifteen

emersyn

"This can't be happening." I've repeated that statement over and over, staring at the front door.

I tick off every moment, every detail of the last hour, searching for the reason he ran out of here like his ass was on fire, but I come up with nothing. Tears pour down my cheeks as the weight of what just happened hits me. I saved myself for Brady. I waited for him to come home and tell me how he felt about me, and against my better judgment, I gave him another chance.

I spent the last year dreaming of how he would tell me he loves me more than anything in this world. Brady promised he was going to do better this time. He promised he was serious this time, and I wanted to believe him. I want to believe that all the emails and sweet text messages over the last month were all real, not just a line he was trying to feed me to get into my pants. He said he was going to prove to me how he felt about me with his actions, not his words. I trusted him, but once again, it seems that I've been tossed to the side like a piece of garbage.

I tried to be careful with my heart, to protect myself from heartbreak a second time. I thought I was keeping my heart guarded from his charm, giving both of us time to get to know each other again. But there was no way for me to protect my heart from Brady. I've loved him for too long and too deeply. I should've known that this was going to happen. All it took was hearing his bullshit sob story, and I crumbled, assuming he'd protect my heart. Cherish it, even. But I was wrong.

"This time was supposed to be different." I crumble to the floor, his cum still dripping down my legs as I give in to my sorrow.

He said that he cared for me and never to doubt his feelings for me. But how else am I supposed to react? The first time he was close to telling me how he felt, he left without a word to fight a war. I'm not heartless, but a simple message in response to my declaration would've been enough. And now he's back in town, doing everything I wanted from him while he was gone. He's responding to my emails, pretending as if my thoughts and feelings matter to him. And I opened my heart and gave Brady the most important gift I had, my virginity, the one thing that I promised myself I would only give to the man I love. But instead of accepting my gift and promising to cherish me forever, he turned his back on me again.

"Nothing can be done. You've had your cry. Now get it together." I push myself up into a sitting position and examine the empty room. I'm alone, in Brady's apartment, for goodness' sake. If I'm going to break down, it won't be here. I have no idea where Brady went, but there's no doubt he'll come back here eventually.

I snatch my shorts off the floor near the door, but there's nothing else. Not a thing out of place. Nothing to even hint about what happened between Brady and me.

"That's a good thing," I choke out, reminding myself of how forgettable I've been to Brady. He left and forgot me two years ago; this time won't be any different.

On top of all that, everyone knows about what has been going on with Brady and me. I haven't kept what's going on between the two of us a secret from my friends, and I would bet money Seth knows since this is his apartment, too. I doubt it would've been very easy to convince him to leave his own apartment without a good reason. And if Seth knows, then Bristol knows, too. If Bristol knows, then Audrey, Selina, and Leia know. And if *they* know, then all the guys know, too. What the hell am I going to tell everyone if they ask how things went? And who am I kidding? They're all so nosy that someone is going to ask, and then I'm going to have to think of something to say that doesn't make me seem like a sex-starved lunatic.

Shit, I can't even imagine how Beckett would react if he had any idea that I came to Brady's house tonight, let alone knew what happened. Beckett has done nothing but try to convince me to stay away from Brady since he caught us kissing in our parents' backyard. He's laid off over the last few weeks, not trying to stick his nose into whatever is going on between Brady and me, but after this...he'll now be public enemy number one in my brother's eyes. The one to blame for anything and everything wrong with me from this day forward.

"I had sex for the first time, and I'm thinking about my older brother..." My voice trails off before laughter comes bubbling out of my mouth like a fucking lunatic, but I can't stop it.

Tears continue to spill down my cheeks. From despair or laughter...who knows? It could be both. The irony of the situation isn't lost on me. Beckett warned me to stay away from Brady, that he would use me and then disappear. And like an idiot, I defended him, telling Beckett that there was no way Brady would treat anyone like that. I bet his head would explode if he found out what happened today, and it's in my best interest for him to never find out.

I lie on my side, trying desperately to stop laughing. To stop crying. To just be. No emotions. No thoughts.

Just nothingness. Time seems to pass, but eventually, my laughter and tears subside. I try to push off the ground, but my arm buckles, sending me tumbling to the floor once again.

"Not this time," I mumble to myself, pushing myself into a sitting position. "First, a shower. I can worry about everything else later."

It's beyond weird to be taking a shower at Brady's place, but I can't bring myself to not clean up. I want to do as much as possible to wash away the physical evidence of what happened between the two of us, but unfortunately, the emotional parts won't wash away so easily. I take a deep breath and push up off the ground, my entire body protesting as I move. My muscles ache from lack of movement, but the pain in my chest is still the most prominent. I shuffle toward the bathroom, using the wall as a guide, all the energy drained from my body. I head directly toward the shower, turning on the hot water full blast, before dropping to the floor as my legs push together, making a squelching sound.

Spreading my legs, I see the creamy liquid tinged with pink collected on my inner things. The only evidence of what Brady stole from me—well, what I gave to him willingly—left. I rip my shirt over my head, desperate to get into the shower, to wash the memories of what could have been down the drain.

"I need to get clean. The last thing I need is someone finding out what happened between us."

Using the side of the tub, I stand before climbing into the shower, then grab the bar of soap and begin scrubbing away all evidence of Brady from my body. I begin with my arms, down to my breasts, and then to my stomach. All areas he caressed, nipped, or sucked on, marking me as his own, never allowing me to give myself in that way to another person, branding me for all eternity. I lift each one of my legs, and a twinge of pain shoots through my body with every movement, reminding me of the way he brought me pleasure like no other.

"He played me," I whisper, breathing life into my thoughts.

I can't help but wonder if Brady Thomas really is the type of man my brother tried to warn me about. I never understood Beckett's sudden change of heart toward his best friend, but maybe he knew something about Brady that I didn't. They were best friends and spent large amounts of time together. Could his sudden overprotectiveness of me be because of that? Because Beckett was afraid that I would be just another pussy, someone to bring Brady pleasure for a short period of time.

No, that can't be right. That's not the type of man Brady is. I don't understand why he ran off like that, but what happened between us meant something to him. He said so himself. I just wish he had stopped to talk to me before running away from me again.

Rage burns through my veins as I shut off the shower, climb out, and grab one of the fluffy towels off the rack. I should probably clean up and try to make it look like nothing happened between Brady and me, but I can't be bothered. I want him to remember what he took from me, to be reminded of what could've been if he had stayed. Right now, my only concern is focusing on putting one foot in front of the other and learning how to live each day without all the pieces of my heart intact.

I wrap the towel around my body, stopping to examine my reflection in the mirror. Angry red marks pepper my cheek and neck from Brady's scruff rubbing repeatedly against my skin, but those should fade soon. My eyes are bloodshot from crying, and a puffiness is setting in under them. But what causes me to pause is the look in them. They're lifeless, as if all the hope I had in the world is gone.

And it's true. I've gone through a torrent of emotions, each one taking hold of me before giving way to the next. Hate, love, sorrow. Each emotion fights for dominance, choking out the last traces of the hope that things with Brady could be different. Right now, the numbness settling around me is what I need. An armor of grief and regret helps me focus on this single moment, no longer worrying about the future, but focusing on the next five minutes, because that's the only way I can move on.

"What am I going to put on?"

Fuck. My only thought was to get cleaned up, but I didn't think about what I could put on. I probably should've grabbed the bag Sophie practically forced me to pack, just in case, but hindsight is twenty-twenty, right? I could go into Brady's room and grab a shirt and some shorts, but that's also out of the question. The last thing I want is anything of his touching my body right now.

I thread my arms through my bra and wrap the towel tighter around my body before I grab my shorts and shirt off the bathroom floor and roll them together into a ball, heading out of the bathroom and across the hall. I peek my head into the room, searching for any traces that this might be Brady's room but find none. After sighing loudly, I pad into the room. This is a total invasion of privacy, but it's an emergency. Thankfully, there is a basket of clothes sitting on the end of the bed. I grab a pair of gray sweatpants and a white T-shirt from the top and pull them on quickly. Both items hanging loosely on my body, way more oversized than I would usually wear, but they work.

"Good enough for government work," I murmur, remembering the phrase Brady has been saying since he joined the military. A pang of loss shoots through me as I start rolling the waistband of the sweats so I can walk and knot the shirt at the waist.

I grab the ball of my clothes off the bed and pad

back down the hallway, looking for a piece of paper or something to write a note on. I search along the table and thankfully find a stray store receipt tucked under a stack of magazines. I scribble Seth a quick note and lay it on top of the basket in his room before heading out the front door.

"Shit," I curse softly, remembering that Sophie dropped me off. I honestly can't think of a good reason why I asked Sophie to drop me off. After spending most of the day primping for my "date" tonight with Sophie and the girls, I asked her to drop me off. I didn't have a good reason at the time other than I didn't want to drive, and I figured Brady wouldn't have an issue dropping me off at my parents' after our date. Sophie and the girls made a big joke out of it, but it wasn't anything I couldn't handle.

But maybe my hesitation to drive myself here should have been the first warning sign of how epically wrong things would go. I came here thinking this was it; it was finally my chance to get the happily ever after with Brady I always dreamed of. However, maybe there was a small part of me that knew something like this would happen, and I'd need my best friend to help me pick up the pieces.

I unball my clothes, sending up a silent prayer that my phone is still in my back pocket. When I reach for the pocket, I sigh in relief and quickly pull out my phone and see a few missed calls from Sophie. Just the person I want to talk to. I hit the *call back* button and wait for her to answer the phone.

"Took you long enough, Emersyn." I roll my eyes, knowing how annoyed she must be if she's using my full name. "You left your bag in my car with the condoms in it. I know you don't plan on getting laid, but better safe than sorry."

Fuck. I didn't even think about that. This would only happen to me, I swear. I lose my virginity and get walked out on. Of course, I was irresponsible and forgot all about using a goddamn condom. *Use a condom. Always use a condom.* It's been drilled into my head since my mom sat me down and had "the talk" at fourteen. Thankfully, my mom also forced me to start taking birth control the week after that talk, "just in case." I've always wanted to have children, but not like this. However, getting pregnant isn't the only thing I have to worry about when having unprotected sex.

Brady made it seem like there hadn't been anyone in his life since our kiss before he left for deployment, but there's a strong possibility that was a lie. I'm going to need to make an appointment with my doctor ASAP just to make sure.

"I need you to come and pick me up," I respond in a monotone voice, hoping Sophie doesn't pick up on the emptiness in my words.

"What happened?"

I should have known better than to call the one

person who can understand my moods. "Nothing. I just need a ride."

"Answer the question, and I'll be on my way."

My armor cracks, but I bite my bottom lip, praying that the pain will keep the sadness out of my voice when I answer. "He left. Just walked out the door and left."

"I'm on my way," she says.

Just like that. No long explanation needed. Those few phrases tell her everything she needs to know. I'm falling apart. I sit on the curb to wait for Sophie, my legs stretched out in front of me and crossed at the ankles. I look around, searching for anything to have changed, but I come up with nothing. Just a heavy sadness sitting in my heart, begging to be released.

"Just a little while longer." I rub at the pain in my chest, waiting for my safe haven to arrive.

Most girls my age would run to their mother or maybe even their siblings to help share their pain, but neither one of them would understand. Sophie is the only person who knows how much Brady has meant to me over the years. She's been the one I've talked to about every email Brady has sent, analyzing every word. If anyone would understand how much it hurts to love the same person for years, waiting for them to see you, it's her. She just knows.

"Hey, babe," Sophie whispers, hopping onto the

trunk of her car beside me. "I hear you had a rough day."

"That would be an understatement," I scoff.

"Want to talk about it?" she prods, not wanting to pry but giving me the chance to put my feelings into words.

"I want to disappear." I sigh. "I want to go someplace that no one would search for me. Just be alone with my thoughts for a few days and figure out how to move forward."

"I've got you covered." She hops off the car and pulls her cell out of her back pocket.

"What are you doing?" I slide off the trunk, wrapping my arms around my waist.

"I'm sending out the bat signal."

I cock my head to the side as she shows me the screen. The words *CHICKEN LITTLE* are on the screen in a group text with Tasha, Rachel, Selina, and Leia. The first three, I understand, but the last person is a mystery to me. I can understand why she would need to text Selina, letting her know I might miss work tomorrow, but why would she need to text Leia?

"What's that supposed to mean?"

"To let the girls know we have an emergency. You need us right this moment, and we need to head over to the cabin Leia keeps ready for our escape from the world."

"Were you three just waiting for this to happen?" I

tilt my head up to the sky and begin blinking rapidly, refusing to cry again. "Waiting for Brady to shatter my heart into a million pieces?"

"Get a grip." Sophie grasps my chin tightly between her fingers and pulls, ensuring I'm looking at her. "We love you."

I pull my chin out of her hold. "Funny way of showing it. Next thing you're going to tell me is you were taking bets on when it was going to happen. Did you win? Were you texting everyone to gloat?"

"I'm going to ignore everything you said for the last minute because I know you aren't this dense." She grabs both of my hands, pulling me toward her for a hug. "We've all been preparing for you to fall apart for two years. You didn't fall apart when he left you without a word. You didn't fall apart when you wrote him letters with no response. Not even a message telling you to fuck off."

I squeeze my best friend tightly as the barrier around my heart shatters into a million pieces, opening the floodgates.

"And now it's all hitting you at once. Every ounce of pain and disappointment at the way Brady has treated you for the last two years and some change. We wanted to ensure that when that happened, you had a safe space to be. To feel everything you're feeling and process without interruption."

"Don't leave me," I beg her, not wanting to be alone

with all these emotions swirling through my body. I need my friends to help me get through this. To show me how to move forward with my head held high. "I need you. All of you." I pull out of her embrace, and she smiles, tears running down her cheeks.

"I know." She grabs my hand, threading her fingers through mine. "Are you ready to go?"

I nod my head, following behind her like a lost child in search of something. What that something is, I have no idea, but what I do know is that everything is going to be okay.

Maybe not right now, but eventually.

I snuggle into my pile of blankets in the California king bed in our cabin tucked into a private corner of Tranquility Retreat. Sophie wasn't kidding when she said they had everything arranged. When we got here about an hour ago, Leia ushered us down toward the river to a secluded two-door cabin.

Apparently, this one is specially reserved for weddings, but since she didn't have anyone coming this weekend, she said it was all ours. Once we were settled in, Sophie called my mom to let her know where we would be for the weekend and then quickly confiscated my phone.

I have no idea what she has planned for me this

weekend, but I'll bet my life that some of it will involve drinking. Drunk Emersyn loves to text and, in some cases, send emails. Could you imagine the trouble I could get into with my phone? Texting Brady and letting him have it would be the least of my worries.

Tasha and Rachel came in about twenty minutes ago with their arms full of anything and everything I could hope to have in my new home away from home: Diet Cherry Coke, Parrot Bay, Malibu, Twizzlers, watermelon Sour Patch Kids, the entire series of *Supernatural* and *Gilmore Girls.* My girls didn't come to play.

"Are you ready to talk yet?" Tasha asks, handing me an unopened package of Twizzlers.

"Can't we watch some *Supernatural* first? I haven't watched 'Yellow Fever' in months."

I look up at her hopefully, but she shakes her head no. I turn toward Rachel, the weakest one in the group.

"Come on, Rach. You know how much better Dean screaming like a little bitch makes me feel."

Rachel giggles softly. "That scene gets me every time."

"Stop stalling." Sophie plops down on the end of the bed, squeezing my feet. "Start talking, or I'm going to run my fingers around your big toe until you do."

"You wouldn't!" I screech as I pull my legs toward my chest.

I made the mistake of telling Sophie how much I

hate having my feet touched, and now she constantly uses it against me. Her own personal brand of torture.

"I would, and you know it." She leans forward, reaching for my feet.

"Okay! Okay!" I throw my hands up in surrender. "I'll talk, but that doesn't mean I have to like it." I snuggle down further into the blankets, only my head peeking out from beneath them. "Brady and I slept together."

"How was it? Did it hurt? Was it everything you imagined it would be and more?" Rachel shoots off rapid-fire questions, getting louder with each one before Sophie pinches her arm. She yelps in surprise, swatting at Sophie before turning her attention back to me. "Sorry. Please continue."

"It was amazing, or at least I thought it was, but the minute Brady realized I was a virgin, he freaked out and left."

"What the shit?" Tasha clasps her hands over her mouth, her eyes flipping back and forth quickly as she realizes what she said.

Tasha hates to curse, but sometimes she can't control herself, and they just slip out, but what makes it even funnier is she never uses them properly.

"I'm going to let that one slide, but only this once, because I want to keep Em talking." Sophie motions for me to continue, trying to hold in her laughter, but she fails, and we all burst into peals of laughter.

I laugh so hard I cry, but as the tears roll down my cheeks, I'm overcome by unbearable sadness, and my laughter quickly turns into wails of pain. Tasha and Rachel wrap me in their arms, holding me tightly as I fall apart. Searing pain flows through my entire body as waves of agony pull me under. I gasp for air, hoping that if I can just hold on a little longer, the pain will subside, and the numbness I've been clinging to for the last few hours will take hold once again, cutting me off from all these feelings that I'm so desperate to forget.

"Make it stop," I whine, clutching my friends like lifelines. "I just want the pain to stop."

"You have to ride the wave, Em," Sophie says. "I know you're hurting right now. But you need to get it out, or it will infect everything that you do, think, or say for the rest of your life. Let it go if you want to heal."

Tears stream down my face as I gasp for breath.

"Did he tell you how he felt about you?" someone asks.

I slam my eyes shut, plunging myself into darkness. Unable to speak, I nod.

"My fault," I choke out. "I-I-knew... I knew...b-but... I believed..."

"Everything will be okay." Tasha gives me a sad smile, but instead of calming me, it ignites a rage inside me.

"Things will never be okay again!" I scream,

pushing out of my friends' embrace and climbing off the bed. "He broke me. Broke! Me!"

I pound my fist into my chest repeatedly.

"Stop." Sophie grabs my wrist, and we struggle for a few moments before she pulls me forward and wraps her arms around me. "Be angry. Be sad. Be whatever it is you need to be, but I'll never let you harm yourself over some dumb asshole who has no idea what he's missing out on."

A gut-wrenching sob escapes me as I bury my face in her neck, snot and tears mixing in her hair as I let my emotions take over. We hold on to each other for the second time today, tears streaming down our cheeks as I attempt to process what has happened in the last twenty-four hours.

Brady has come home from war. After not seeing him for two years, we ran into each other at the bar a month ago. *Holy crap. Has it really only been a month?* He thinks I've got a boyfriend and suddenly wants to make things right between us. He fixes my car and is prepared to sweep me off my feet. He talks to my brother and starts responding to my emails, but has anything really changed between us? Suddenly, everything makes sense.

There's no excuse for Brady's behavior, in the past or today, but maybe he's just as confused as I am. From what my mom has said, he's just retired from the same life he's had since he graduated from high school. He has to adjust to being home, having a nine-to-five job, and finding a place to live. All things that I've been doing my entire life, but they are all new to him. He also has spent the last two years pretending to feel nothing for me because of his own insecurities and feelings of inadequacy. All of that was bullshit, but he didn't believe that. He had no idea I didn't feel that way until I told him.

Is it possible that he's just as overwhelmed and lost as I am right now? No, there's no excuse for what he did to me, but there could be a reason for it.

I step out of Sophie's embrace. "I'm okay now. Well, as okay as I can be." I grab her hand before turning toward my other two friends. "Thank you for being here. For dropping anything you had going on in your life to help me stop mine from falling apart."

"What are friends for?" Tasha says with a smile.

"No. Sisters," Rachel chimes in, bumping Tasha's shoulder before throwing an arm over it and pulling her in for a one-armed hug.

That's right, we're sisters. Although not by blood, I'm closer to these three girls than to anyone in this world, including my brother.

"Emersyn?" Tasha climbs out of the bed, grabbing my free hand and squeezing.

"Yes?"

Sophie holds her hand out to Rachel, inviting her to join our circle. She smiles brightly before climbing off of the bed and grasping both Sophie's and Tasha's other hands.

"I know this isn't what you want to hear right now, but I'm sure Brady has a reason for what he did. He isn't the type to just run out on someone he cares for," Tasha says, as she drops her head to my shoulder.

A dark laugh bubbles from my throat. "Save it. This isn't the first time he's run out on me. Just the most recent, and it's so much worse. I don't think there's anything he can ever say to me to explain leaving me like that. I get it. He chickened out."

"She's right," Sophie chimes in.

Rachel nods her head in agreement. "People change, but has he really changed that much? He's spent the last month trying to find a way to help you understand why he blew you off during deployment. He never made an excuse for his actions; he owned them and has been trying to make it up to you ever since."

I take a moment to contemplate what she's saying. Brady and I were attached at the hip before he was deployed, but he wrote in his emails that he never thought he was good enough for me. That he joined the Marines so he had a chance of being able to take care of me, to give me everything I ever wanted. But he never bothered to ask me what I wanted. I didn't need a big house or to be able to travel around the world. The only thing I want most in the world is him.

Sophie squeezes my hand to get my attention. I turn and find her eyes pleading with me to listen to what she is saying, but I don't know how. What type of justification could the man have for ripping my heart to shreds a second time? First, two years ago, leaving me without any hope that he returned my feelings, and now, when he poured his heart out to me. He told me he loved me and wanted to spend the rest of his life making me happy before running out on me after I gave him the single most precious gift I could give to anyone.

The worst thing of all is that he gave me a glimpse of how things could've been between us. An idea of what the world would be like if he loved me as much as I loved him. The moment he wrapped me in his arms after fixing my car, I knew I was a goner. I tried to protect my heart and shield myself from the potential heartbreak the moment I let him back in, but I fell for it all, hook, line, and sinker.

"What if I said you don't understand the type of man Brady is?" Sophie asks.

"And you do?" I throw my hands up in the air. "I thought you were on my side."

I walk away from my friends, plopping down on the bed and clutching a pillow to my chest.

"I am." Sophie rolls her eyes before sinking down on the bed beside me. "And that's why I won't let you make an emotional decision that you'll regret later."

"What kind of friends would be if we let you do

that?" Rachel chimes in, climbing onto the bed and wrapping her arms around my neck, giving me a hug from behind.

"You agree with her?" I squeeze Rachel's hand, showing her my thanks. One can never get too many hugs.

"I don't agree or disagree with anyone. But I do have to admit that what she's saying makes sense. Maybe you should ask him what's going on before writing him off forever."

"What about you?" I motion for Tasha to join us on the bed.

She's my only hope for hearing what I want to hear.

"I think there's a piece of the puzzle that you're missing." She shakes her head, opening her mouth to speak, but stopping.

"Okay, enough. I'm not shutting down or trying to hide from my problem, but I don't want to think about it anymore." My shoulders sag in defeat.

That's one thing about my friends: they never tell me what I *want* to hear, but what I *need* to hear in order to move on. And it always gives me a lot to think about. However, thinking is the last thing I want to do right now.

"Can't we just watch some *Supernatural* or whatever else you ladies brought along with you, eat our weight in junk food, and pretend for the weekend that nothing else exists?"

Tasha smirks in response. "Sure can, but we aren't skipping episodes. It's been a while since I've had a chance to rewatch the show since the series ended. We pick a season and watch the whole thing."

"Deal, but we are not watching season eight. That's my least favorite," I concede, knowing she wasn't ready for my answer.

If she won't let me watch them the way I want, then neither can she.

"But Charlie!" Tasha and Rachel screech in unison.

Sophie lets out a loud laugh. "You won't let us skip episodes, so no season eight."

She crosses her arms over her chest, feeling the same way as me. This is an age-old argument between the four of us, hence the reason we haven't rewatched the entire series.

"Fine." Rachel flops back down on the bed, her eyes lighting with mischief. "But then we're playing a drinking game while we watch."

"Now you're speaking my language." Sophie rubs her hands together, grabs one of the boxes, and heads toward the television.

"I hope we got enough Diet Coke," Tasha responds, digging into the bags of supplies they brought for our weekend getaway.

I just smile, knowing that with these three by my side, I can get through anything.

sixteen

brady

Things with Emersyn and me are a complete mess. I should have stayed and at least explained to her what was going on with me, but I took off like the coward I am. I can't even imagine how she felt when I left without a word, not that I've spoken to her since then.

After grabbing us both some burgers and dessert from the diner, I climbed into my truck and started driving. I didn't have a specific destination in mind; I just drove around town, trying to clear my head. I thought I'd gotten Beckett's voice from that night out of my head. That I'd come to terms with the fact that Emersyn chose me. She loves me. Not the things I can buy or do for her, but me as a man. That's all she's ever asked me for, but in that moment, I felt like everything Beckett said about me was the truth, and I ran.

After getting my shit together enough, I headed back to my apartment, praying she'd still be there and allow me to explain everything, but she was gone. I sent her a quick text wanting to make sure she was safe, but I didn't get a response. I can't say I blame her for not responding or leaving. I deserted her again, and in the worst way possible. I should have stayed with her, drawn her a bath, and tucked her into my bed. But instead, I ran away, just like I did two years ago.

It's only been a few days, and my heart aches like someone has ripped it out of my chest. Until this moment, I couldn't understand Seth's issue with Bristol giving him the cold shoulder and not responding to his texts or calls, but now I understand. He wasn't being clingy, wanting to know her every move. He wanted to be a part of it. The small tidbits of Bristol's life that she shares with him make his day, bringing them closer with each passing day. They aren't the same people they were before we left for deployment. The spark between them is still there, but there is no way they could just pick up where things left off. They need to take the time to get to know each other better, in order to ensure that this time they stay together.

That's what I wanted to tell Emersyn at our dinner. I promised to prove to her that I deserved to be a part of her life. That we deserve the chance to see where things could go between us, with no one getting in our way. I understand that now more than ever. I've let her brother's words get to me again, placing doubts in my mind, telling me I wasn't good enough for her and I didn't even deserve to breathe the same air as her. And

I'm *not* good enough, especially after deserting her like that again, that's for sure. But that doesn't mean I can't be with her. I will do anything, give up anything, for the chance to spend every day of my life with her. But first, I need to get her to talk to me. Not an easy task, by any means, but I need to at least try.

Shaking the dark thoughts from my mind, I pull a jacket over my long-sleeved shirt and make sure Seth has everything ready for his surprise tonight.

"You ready for today?" I ask him.

"I think so. Your mom is dropping off the pie she made around dinnertime and will make sure everything is good to go before Bristol and I get there." He pats me on the back before grabbing his keys off the hook. "Thanks, man. I don't think I would have been able to pull any of this off without your help."

Vance invited the whole crew over to celebrate with him and Selina today, and Seth thought this would be the best opportunity to take his relationship with Bristol to the next level. Bristol was concerned about Seth not having roots, worried that he would just bail whenever he felt like it, but he wanted to show her he was here to stay. I say buying a house and joining the local sheriff's department with my dad is a step in the right direction.

The guys and I spent the last few days helping Seth get his new house ready for tonight. Thankfully, there wasn't much to do, and since Audrey moved in with

Connor, Seth grabbed a few pieces of furniture from her for a decent price to make the place feel more like home.

"Just name your firstborn after me and we can call it even." I wink, heading down the stairs toward the truck and climbing in.

"Are you sure you want to do this tonight?" I ask as he climbs in.

Seth rolls his eyes at me. "Yes, I'm sure. More time won't change my feelings for Bristol. I need her to know I'm here for the long haul. Showing her my place and telling her how much I love her is the first step in that direction."

Bristol and Seth haven't known each other for very long. Not that I doubt how much he loves her. Listening to him whine about her during deployment helped convince me about love at first sight. But what if she doesn't feel the same way and would rather remain friends?

My fears about Emersyn kicking me to the curb for good filter through my mind. I don't want to ruin Seth's day with my negative thoughts, but I need to know why he's so sure this is the right thing to do.

"But you can only do this once, man. You said yourself that she's been holding something back from you. What happens if it's something bigger than you can imagine?"

I'm not trying to convince Seth it's something serious. A secret is a secret. However, I can't help but wonder if it is. I've tried to bring it up with the guys and even my mom a few times, but each time, I get shut down. I tried to convince Seth to ask, but he has always seemed unfazed. How is he not the least bit concerned about what it could be? How is he ready to surge full steam ahead with her after only such a short period of time?

"I need to do this. For both our sakes," he says with conviction.

"All right, man. Whatever you need, I'm here for you," I respond before turning my attention toward the window. "I didn't mean to let my issues rain on your parade."

"I've been so wrapped up in my shit, I haven't been there for you," he apologizes as he starts his truck and pulls out of the driveway. We drive in silence for a few minutes before he speaks again. "I found an interesting note in my laundry basket from Emersyn about borrowing some clothes."

Fuck. Shame fills my body as the memories of what happened that night fill my system. I could tell him the truth about what happened, but I don't have it in me to listen to one of his lectures. "Yeah, she came over to hang out the other night."

"Is that why you told me to find a couch to sleep on?" He chuckles softly as we turn onto Vance and

Selina's street. "Troy's couch is very comfortable, in case you were wondering."

Vance and Selina's house is a little further out from town, being closer to the river, but it's worth the drive. Most people are knocking these old houses down to make room for cookie-cutter housing developments, but these two had a different idea. Vance and Connor renovated this entire house, turning it into Selina's dream home.

"I wasn't, actually," I grumble, turning my attention out the window, hoping Seth would just drop it.

"So, what did she need the clothes for? Couldn't she have just borrowed something from you? You're much closer to her size than I am."

"Yeah, maybe, but she went into the wrong room," I choke out, fighting against the waves of regret washing over me.

I wish I could turn back the clock and change almost everything about that night. I don't regret having sex with Emersyn. Do I regret that our first time together was against my front door? Yes, of course. But I could never regret Emersyn giving me the honor of bestowing me with such a special gift. I do regret how I acted. I freaked out and left her in my apartment alone, probably in pain, and most certainly confused. If I could change anything, it would be that. Instead of running, I'd have carried her to the bathroom and run a warm bath for her. I'd have cleaned every inch of her, following the washcloth with my lips as I whispered how much I loved her. After she was all clean, I'd have wrapped her in a warm towel before lifting her a second time and carrying her into my room.

How different things would be right now if I had been able to keep my shit together and think about her before running. I've told her a million times I would show her how much she means to me, and at my first opportunity, I blew it.

"I wish I had it all figured out like you." I sigh. "Everything has changed since I came home. It was changing before I even enlisted. Walker and Riggs went off to college and made a life for themselves away from Tyson's Creek. By the time I came home from my last deployment, Vance and Connor had Ace & Hammer. Everyone moved on to bigger and better things, but I'm still stuck in the same place. I still live in the small apartment above my parents' garage."

"There's nothing wrong with any of that, Brady. We all take different paths in life, but that doesn't make any of our choices better than the other, just different."

I scoff, turning my attention out the window. "Even you're leaving me behind."

"What do you mean?"

"You're leaving me behind, just like everyone else. I'm happy for you, don't get me wrong. You deserve to be with the woman you love, but you just made the decision and stuck with it. No detours or stops along the way. You've been full steam ahead since the moment you decided to make Tyson's Creek your new home, while I can't do anything but continue to mess up."

All my thoughts and feelings over the last few months come pouring out of me, and I can't stop them. I've spent so long with all these emotions bottled up inside me that it was inevitable I'd blow at some point. I just didn't know when.

I'm floundering big time. I want to make a life for myself, something that is only mine, but I've yet to find that. I have a job that was given to me, a place to live that my parents pay for, and a relationship that was doomed before it started. What do I have to offer anyone, let alone Emersyn? She's spent the last two years of her life waiting for me to come back to her, to tell her how I feel, and I did that. But my fears got the better of me. The voices inside my head kept telling me that I'd never amount to anything or be able to carve a place in the world of my own, holding me back from taking what's mine.

"Everyone else is moving on with their lives and finding the one thing in the world they can call their own but me. And I'm holding Emersyn back with me. I know I should let her go because everything is different now, but I can't. The idea of not having her in my life causes a piece of my soul to die every time I think about it but, what do I have to offer her?"

"Love," Seth responds with conviction. "Your love. If she truly loves you, that's all she wants. That's all she has ever wanted from you. Not gifts or a fancy house. I bet she'd be happy living in a cardboard box, as long as you two were together."

"What if that isn't enough? What if I'm not enough?"

There it is. My biggest fear laid out for the world to see. I've always felt like I wasn't enough. It was never any one thing that happened, but a combination of things that have piled up on top of each other over the years. Tests I didn't do well on, jobs I was turned down for, all leading to the day my best friend in the world told me he would never allow me near his sister. He was protecting her, sure, but what type of man would be good enough for her? I've spent the last two years trying to become that man, but the reality is I already was.

Emersyn didn't want me to become someone I wasn't; she wanted me. I can see that now, but before I left on deployment—hell, even only a few days ago—the voices were too loud, and I panicked. It seems only natural that something like this would happen. My entire world has been flipped upside down. I've gone from someone telling me when to eat and sleep, what to wear, and even how to properly groom myself for over half my life to being responsible for every aspect of my life.

It's quite possible that after I left her alone in my apartment, she changed her mind. That she's sick of my shit and ready to move on with her life, but I can't let her go. I need to find some way to apologize or at least explain to her why I did what I did. I don't have an excuse but an explanation. I'm not the same man she fell in love with, and I may never be that man again. I don't know when or how it happened, but I let my insecurities take over my mind.

Beckett's words begin playing on repeat in my mind, but I shake my head. He's right about me not being good enough for Emersyn, but I plan to spend the rest of my life trying to be better. I'm not leaving. I'm not running away from her again because I need her like I need my next breath.

"You're still the same person you were before we went over to the sandbox." Seth chuckles while shaking his head. "The same person she fell in love with. But something's holding you back."

"I never said she was in love with me. Besides, what the hell does she know about love? She's barely lived life yet. What if she just thinks she's in love with me, like everyone has been saying?" I mumble, not wanting to get my hopes up.

Emersyn told me she loved me two years ago. I can't help but hope she's read every email I've sent her, allowing me the chance to show her how I feel about her. She's given me numerous chances to show her how much I love her. And then she chose to sleep with me, to allow me the honor of being the first person to love her in that way, and I threw it away like it meant nothing. I did the exact thing I promised her I'd try to never do again because I was afraid. How the hell can I ever expect her to give me another chance after walking away from her? Again. How does love survive something like that? I know the saying is *love conquers all*, but does it really?

"Any woman who's still waiting around for your ass after this long is in love with you," Seth insists.

I turn my head to the side, my shoulders slumping in defeat. It seems as if everything I've ever dreamed of in my life has disappeared, leaving me with nothing but regret.

"What is it you said to me about Bristol? Everyone knows Emersyn loves you. Now you just need to prove to her that you're worthy of her love."

I don't respond, climbing out of the truck without a word, but Seth's words give me hope. She may not still love me now, but there's no saying she can't fall in love with me again. I need to beg for her forgiveness a second time and try and do better. I've told her I would mess up again, but she needs to know why I keep doing these things. That these feelings have become an ingrained part of me and won't easily be changed, but I'm willing to try for her. I'm willing to become a better man for both of us. I'm human and make mistakes, but that doesn't mean my feelings for her have changed. I'm in love with Emersyn, but I let the little nagging voice in the back of my head get to me, forgetting that the only person who can deem me unworthy is her.

I throw my arm over Seth's shoulder as he comes around the front of the truck and smiles. "Enough about me. It's time for you to go claim your girl."

I have no idea what the future holds for me, but as long as Emersyn is in it, I'm content.

seventeen

brady

"Can I get a beer?" I ask Sherry as I take a seat at the bar.

Crawdaddy's is the last place I expected to be. I should be home, trying to think of a way to get Emersyn back, but after everything Seth went through this past weekend, I'm seeing everything in a new light.

Bristol was hiding one major secret: a baby. That's right, a baby. It seems Seth left Bristol with a little more than just his heart and the hope he'd come home. Seth overheard her and the girls talking, and it blew up from there. I don't know what he's going to do, but he has a lot to think about, as do I.

After he stormed away from Vance's house, I got the story about what happened. Thankfully, I had no idea about any of it, or I would have been on Seth's shit list, as well. All the relationships he was building here were a lie, at least in his eyes. He didn't understand why they would keep such a huge secret from him. The kicker was, he wasn't angry about having a daughter he knew nothing about. More than anything, he was hurt that no one thought he could handle knowing. That he would bounce and never return, breaking Bristol's heart all over again.

I can't say I blame them, but I know Seth. I know how he pined for her while we were overseas, yearning for the day he'd have her in his arms again. I can't help but find some similarities between Bristol's actions and mine. She was afraid of what he would think or feel if he knew the truth. That he would come back to her because of their daughter, not because he was in love with her.

"What brings you here in the middle of the day?" Sherry places a bottle of some imported beer in front of me.

I reach into my back pocket to grab my wallet, but she holds up her hand. "Your money's no good here."

I smirk. "It's not like that anymore."

Things are different now. Beckett and I aren't as close as we used to be. I don't think we ever will be after what happened with Emersyn. Emersyn and I are different. We aren't the same people we were before I left. She has made a life for herself both in Tyson's Creek and at school. She has friends that adore her, and I don't want to be the person holding her back. I have issues of my own to deal with, ones that I had long before joining the military, and a few that crept up along the way. Things that if I don't get a handle on could ruin any chance of Emersyn and me being together. Damn, I don't even know if there's anything between us anymore since I haven't spoken to her since that night in my apartment. I've been racking my brain for a way to get her to speak to me, and that's how I ended up here.

However, I'm not looking forward to telling Beckett I did the exact thing I promised I wouldn't do a second time: I broke his sister's heart. But I'm desperate. If there is any hope of Emersyn and me finding our way back to each other a second time, I'm going to need his help.

Emersyn hasn't answered any of my texts or calls since Friday afternoon, not that I blame her. Walking out on someone after you have sex for the first time is a dick move. Add in all our other baggage, and I'll be surprised if she ever speaks to me again. But I have to try. I'll get on my hands and knees to beg for forgiveness if I need to. Anything to make up for the way I've treated her these past two years. No one deserves to feel unloved, especially when she has become the air I breathe.

I want to blame Beckett for the mess I'm in now, but it's not his fault. He has just become the face of my insecurities, but he isn't the cause. I doubt he even knows anything about them because we don't really spend time talking about our feelings. We're men, and men are supposed to be strong. We are never supposed to feel insecure or worry about what other people think of us, or it will make us seem less "manly" to the rest of the world. At least that's what my therapist said to me during our last talk.

Yeah, a therapist. I never thought I'd be willing to go and talk to someone, let alone a stranger, about my feelings. But if I want to become a better man for Emersyn, I need to make sure this never happens again. I need to find a way to get the voices inside of me under control.

"Whatever happened between the two of you, anyway? Thick as thieves, and then right before you left, cold turkey." She shakes her head. "If I didn't know any better, I'd say it was about a girl."

I tip my beer in her direction. "You got it."

Sherry leans forward, both elbows on the bar. "You've got to be kidding me. Did you make a move on Sophie?"

I chuckle softly. It's no secret how infatuated Sophie is with Beckett, but I had no idea her feelings were reciprocated.

"Last time I checked, he didn't even know she existed," I remark.

"A lot has changed since you left."

"You can say that again," I mumble before taking a swig from the bottle in my hand.

"Sounds like you came in here for a lot more than

just a beer." She smiles. "It's in my job description as a bartender. I'm a good listener if you just want an ear."

"Thanks, but you're not the person I need to talk to."

She nods toward the back of the bar. "He's in his office."

I'm not exactly sure what I'm going to say to Beckett, but he needs to understand what is going on with me, the effect his words and actions have had on both me and Emersyn, and that I'm also in love with his sister. I'm working on myself so I can be better for her, but it's going to take time for me to get there. I need him to understand that we will have ups and downs in our relationship, good times and bad times, but we need to be given the chance to work through them. I know that Beckett loves his sister and wants nothing more than to protect her from being hurt, but Emersyn is a grown woman who can make her own decisions. I just hope one of those decisions is agreeing to give us a shot, even if her brother has issues with it.

"Here goes nothing," I mumble to myself before taking a breath and knocking on the office door.

"Come in." Beckett's gruff voice filters through the door.

I push it open and step inside. Not much has changed around Beckett's office since the last time I was back here. A large wooden desk, piled high with papers and magazines, sits in the middle of the room.

Beckett has never been the most organized person in a conventional sense. More like organized chaos. Everything has its place here, not that anyone else would be able to understand that.

A large window takes up more of the left wall, looking down onto the bar below. On the right is a large pull-out couch pushed up against the wall, and photos of everyone important in his life hang on the walls.

"You really made this place a home away from home," I murmur, breaking the silence.

Beckett says nothing, his nose still buried in the papers before him. It seems I'm going to have to work harder to get him to chat with me.

"I can't believe you still have this old thing," I chuckle, flopping down onto the dilapidated piece of furniture.

"If it's not broke, don't fix it, right?" he mutters, not even bothering to look in my direction. "What are you doing here?"

"Can't I stop by and say hello?"

"Not when my sister has been held up somewhere all weekend with her phone shut off after going to have dinner with you." Beckett swings around in his chair, pinning me in place with his stare.

I sigh, running my hand through my hair as I try to come up with an answer that isn't going to get me punched but come up empty.

"What the fuck did you do to my sister, Brady?" he deadpans, his eyes locking with mine for the first time.

"I left. Again," I respond, cutting right to the heart of the situation. "I asked her to come over for dinner, but I didn't know that she..."

"Don't finish that fucking sentence," Beckett growls, his entire body shaking in anger.

Shit. I only planned on telling him that I left Emersyn again, without any idea of what was going through my mind. Not that we slept together. I know I didn't say that in so many words, but Beckett's smart. He put two and two together.

"Let me get this straight. You promised you'd never treat her like that. You told me you loved her more than your own life."

"Yes."

"I gave you an in with my sister against my better judgment, and then you...you slept with her and FUCKING LEFT!" he roars, his arms sweeping across the desk. All the papers, magazines, and books crash to the floor, making the already chaotic room even more of a mess. "I'm going to fucking end you."

Beckett storms toward me, hands clenched tightly by his side. I stand to my full height, I barely come up to his chin, but I refuse to back down. Beckett needs to understand that I'm not giving up on Emersyn. "I fucked up, Beckett. I know that, and I need a chance to apologize to her. I need your help."

His eyes widen in disbelief as he pulls back his arm and gives me a well-placed right hook to the jaw. I stumble backward, rotating my jaw. "I deserve that, but you're not going to get another free shot.

"Ever since we graduated from high school, I've never felt like I was good enough for anyone, let alone Emersyn. You, Walker, and Riggs were moving forward with your lives, and I felt like I was standing still. I've been desperately in love with Emersyn for a few years now. I know you knew, and I wanted to prove to myself that I could take care of her, even though I was in the Marines."

Beckett stares at me with nothing but pure malice in his eyes, but he doesn't try to hit me again, so I take that as a good sign to continue.

"But no matter how hard I worked, all I could hear was your voice in my head telling me to stay away from her. That I'd never be good enough for her. You managed to tap into every one of my insecurities and use them to your advantage."

"How was I supposed to know..." His eyebrows pull down in confusion as his voice trails off.

"You were—*are* one of my best friends, Beckett. Every time I asked you what I could do to convince you I was good enough for her, what you would need from me to know if I could take care of her...I did each and every thing you asked of me, but every time I could check one thing off the list, you added another one.

And then when you couldn't think of anything else, you blamed the Marines."

"So, this is *my* fault?" He chuckles darkly, taking another swing at me, but I step back, and he barely misses connecting with my chin a second time. "It's my fault you fucked my sister and ran away like a pussy?"

"I never said that, but yes, you had something to do with it. I have my own problems I need to work through, but you need to stop trying to sabotage our relationship. If she'll forgive me, I'm going to spend the rest of my life working to be a better man. Not just for her, but for both of us."

I can tell by the look in Beckett's eyes that he's expecting me to back down like I did in the past, but he has another thing coming. This time, I plan on fighting for Emersyn, taking down anything standing in my way. Including him, if need be.

"How is now any different? First, you left her in our parents' backyard without a word, and this time, you..." His voice trails off slightly before he begins again. "Give me one good reason why I should let you anywhere near my baby sister again."

"I love her," I say without hesitation, my eyes locked with his. "I left the party at your parents' house because I needed to think through what was going on, and then I deployed. I couldn't do anything about that. But this time, I was afraid. There's no excuse for how I reacted. All the voices telling me I wasn't good enough and she deserved better were ringing loudly in my ear, and I ran. I own that, but I'm here, begging you to help me find a way to talk to her."

"You plan on fighting for her this time? I know I fucked up and put myself between you two before you left for deployment, but I didn't expect you to take my words as gospel and walk away from her." Beckett stands, breathing heavily from our altercation.

"How could you not? You were my best friend and her older brother. Family is everything to Emersyn. There was no way we could ever be together if you were constantly getting in our way."

He stumbles backward, his knees buckling as he flops down onto the couch. "I was trying to protect my sister."

"From me?"

"From everyone!" He drops his chin to his chest before threading his fingers through his hair and tugging on it. "I've told you before, no one will ever be good enough for her!"

My ears perk at the sound of the door opening.

"I've tried keeping you two apart and paid the price more than once," he continues, oblivious to the sound. "I never want to see the look of pure devastation on her face again. A look that you've put there both times. So, tell me, what the fuck do you plan on doing about it?"

"Isn't this fucking rich?" We freeze at the sound of

Emersyn's voice, thick with hurt and anger. "You leave me standing in your apartment all alone, but I find you come to my brother to ask for forgiveness before speaking to me?"

I hold my hands to the side, walking toward her cautiously. Her entire body trembles, her head swiveling from side to side, trying to make sense of what she just overheard. "That's not what's going on, Em."

"Don't fucking *Em* me, Brady!"

"Emersyn." Beckett takes a step toward her, but she steps back out of the room.

"Do you know what happened?" She sniffles, tears pooling in her eyes.

I want to wrap her in my arms and whisper in her ear that everything will be okay, but I'm the last person in the world she wants to be near right now.

"Yes," he says softly. "But he came here to ask for a chance to explain. He knew that I could help him get in contact with you."

"I've texted and called you nonstop since that night. I left because I was afraid."

"*Afraid?* What the fuck did you have to be afraid of? If anyone should've been afraid, it was me. But for some dumb reason, I believed you. I believed every word you wrote to me in those emails."

"I meant every word, Emersyn. I also told you about how I felt like I wasn't good enough for you. That no matter how hard I tried, I always felt that I couldn't give you what you deserved."

"But I told..." she begins, but I cut her off.

"I know you did, but that doesn't change the way that I feel, does it?"

"And I only made things worse. I can see that now." Beckett's shoulders drop in defeat. "I was so focused on protecting you from being hurt that I took away your choice. I made him believe that you would be better off if he wasn't in your life. That he'd be holding you back, forcing you to spend your entire life following him around and never having a life of your own."

I reach my hand toward her, wanting to comfort her in some way, but I don't. My arms drop to my side as I shove my hands into my pockets. My hands ball into fists as I fight the urge to touch her. "He only wanted to protect you," I say softly, wanting to help her understand where her brother was coming from. "He loves you more than anything in this world. It may have been misplaced, but Beckett wasn't trying to hurt either of us."

"He was trying to protect me from you." She rolls her eyes as she strides further into the room, stopping a few inches away from me. "And in light of recent events, I'm starting to believe he had a good reason."

She doesn't spare me a glance before making a beeline for her brother. "Let me tell you something, Beckett James Carter. I've said this a million times, but maybe it will actually make it through your thick skull this time. I'm an adult, and I can make my own decisions and mistakes. That's how we grow, asshole!" Her finger smashes into his chest with every phrase, and then she spins around, turning her anger at me. "And you. I love you with all my heart and would have follo

wed you to the ends of the earth. But after the other day, I don't even know if you understand what it means to love someone."

"I do, Em. I knew the minute I left my apartment I had fucked up, but all the voices in my head wouldn't shut up. I went to the diner to grab food for us to eat, hoping when I got back, we could talk things out. I foolishly thought you'd still be there waiting for me, giving me another chance to explain myself. I'm so sorry, Emersyn."

She swipes at the angry tears trailing down her cheeks. "Sorry isn't going to cut this time. From either of you."

"I *am* sorry," I tell her.

She opens her mouth to respond, but I step closer, pulling her into my chest.

"I'm an idiot. I thought that I had all my insecurities and negative voices inside my head under control. But they weren't. In that moment, I felt like I wasn't good enough for you. Those feelings suffocated me, reminding me of all the ways I was letting you down.

And instead of talking to you, explaining to you what I was thinking and feeling, I ran. And I'm sorry."

I bury my nose in her hair and inhale deeply, allowing her scent to calm my nerves. "I've been talking to a therapist. I need to find a way to regain control of my life, but it will take some time. I already told you I knew I'd fuck up again, and this was the ultimate fuckup, but I'm trying to do better. To be a better man for you."

"Prove it," she scoffs, nuzzling her nose into my chest.

I can hear the conviction in her words as she steps out of my embrace.

"I need to know that you won't shatter my world to pieces like that again. I know you say you're sorry, but actions speak louder than words."

I nod, my arms dropping to my sides.

"Stay the hell away from my sister until you figure your shit out, asshole," Beckett growls, stepping around me to get to Emersyn.

"Oh, no. Don't think your ass is off the hook." She points toward him. "You are my brother, but it's not your responsibility to protect me from the world. Love me, be a shoulder for me to cry on when I need it, but I don't need protecting."

She spins on her heels to leave but pauses, looking over her shoulder at the both of us. "Just give me some time, both of you. I understand that what you did was out of some misplaced sense of love, but I need time to work through all of this. Having both of you breathing down my neck won't help matters at all."

I smile softly at her before nodding my head in confirmation. I assume Beckett does the same as she heads out the door. Beckett and I remain silent as her footsteps echo through the hall.

"She isn't a little girl anymore, is she?" Becket mumbles, causing me to chuckle.

"We've been trying to tell you that."

"You're really going to therapy?" he questions, his eyes still focused on the door.

"Yes. I didn't think I needed it at first, but after what happened with Emersyn, I knew something had to change. I called the Veteran Crisis Hotline that very night and talked to someone. I've had a standing appointment once a week since that night."

"You'd really do anything to make my sister happy, wouldn't you?"

"That's what I've been trying to tell you. I love her more than my own life. I'll always be by her side, trying to be better, until she orders me away."

Beckett flops back down onto the couch, resting his head on the back of it. "I know I said this before, but I really do need more time to wrap my head around the idea of you two being more than just friends."

"Understandable." I stoop down, gathering papers off the floor.

"Leave it. I can take care of it later."

"You sure?" I lay the stack in my hands on the end of the desk and turn toward him.

"Yeah. Get out of here before I sock you in the jaw again."

"Lucky shot." I chuckle before turning and heading out the door.

As I wave goodbye to Sherry, there's a pep in my step.

Things with Beckett and I won't be the same for a while, but I think he finally understands where I'm coming from. He's been my best friend for years, and though I doubt we'll ever be that close again, this is a step in the right direction.

As for Emersyn? She has a small inkling of how I feel about her, but she needs proof that I won't do anything like that again. I need to do something that will prove to her beyond a shadow of a doubt that she's it for me, and I know just the woman to ask for help.

eighteen

brady

"Hey, Ma!" I shout as I come barreling through the door.

I spent the entire drive home wracking my brain, trying to come up with an idea of how to prove to Emersyn how much she means to me, and I may have come up with the perfect plan.

"What are you screaming for?" My mother rounds the corner to the kitchen. "What's so important?"

"I need your help." I plop down into a chair at the kitchen table, dropping my head into my hands. "I messed up big time."

I have no idea how I'm going to explain to my mother what happened with Emersyn without giving her more details than either of us wants shared with the world, let alone our parents.

"Sounds serious." She lays her hand on my shoulder, giving it a squeeze. "Tell me what happened."

My mother has always been there for me, knowing what I need even before I do sometimes. I know that no matter what I tell her, she'll be angry, but there is no way she is going to let me walk out of this kitchen until we've found a solution to my problem.

"I'm in love with Emersyn."

She snickers. "We all know that, honey. I'm glad you've finally gotten with the program."

"I know I'm a little late to the game, but I messed up."

I grip the back of my neck, dreading having to tell her what an asshole I've been, but she needs to know exactly how badly I may have ruined things with Emersyn.

She looks at me skeptically for a few moments. "How bad?"

I wince, knowing she is going to give me the what-for once I tell her what happened. "She told me she loved me before I left for deployment, but I freaked out and ran."

She opens and closes her mouth a few times before speaking again. "Is that it?"

I shake my head. "She wrote to me throughout my entire deployment, sending packages or anything she could to let me know she was still here thinking about me, but I didn't respond to any of them."

"Oh, dear Lord above. Brady Michael Thomas, if you weren't almost twice my size, I would take you over my knee right now and tan your hide."

"I'm sorry, Momma, but it gets worse."

My mom pushes away from the table and heads into the kitchen. I hear her mumbling something to herself as the cabinets open and shut loudly.

"You all right in there, Ma?" I ask, trying to judge if it's going to be a glass of wine or whiskey she comes back with.

If it's wine, I may get out of this situation unscathed, but if she comes back with the bottle of whiskey stashed in the back of the pantry, I'm in trouble. Debbie Thomas isn't a drinker by any means, but sometimes she needs something to calm her nerves. What she chooses depends on how badly I've ruffled her feathers.

"Shit," I mutter under my breath as she comes back with a bottle of whiskey and two glasses.

"Don't use that tone with me, Brady." She places the glasses on the table, pouring a healthy amount into each of them before taking a seat. "Okay. Continue."

I grab my glass and take a sip, hoping the liquid will calm my nerves. Instead, it feels as if molten lava is being poured down my throat.

I wince. "Man, that burns."

My mom snickers, taking a sip from her glass like a champ. "You need a little more practice, son. This will put hair on your chest and is much better than that watered-down beer you boys drink every day."

"There's a time and place for hard liquor, Ma." I

raise my glass in her direction. "Today happens to be one of those days."

She nods before taking another sip and smiling. "So, tell me what you've done to this poor girl."

I take a deep breath and brace myself for the dressing-down I'm about to get from my mother. "When I came home, I had every intention of telling her how I felt, but things haven't gone as planned. I ended up hurting her more." I take another sip, the burning now just a dull ache in my throat. "And then I went to Crawdaddy's today to ask Beckett to help, and he punched me, but we talked it out. However, she walked in on said conversation and gave both of us the what-for."

"Good for her," my mom responds before swallowing the last of her glass and slamming it down on the table. "I had a feeling something like this was going to happen. Beckett has always been protective of his sister. A little too much, if you ask me. I always thought with you two being so close, he would ease up, but I see that wasn't the case."

"Yeah, he did everything he could to get between us, and I let him. He got into my head, taking all my insecurities and throwing them back in my face."

"Brady, we all make mistakes. It's what makes us human. It's how we choose to make amends that matters."

I smile at my mother, grabbing her hand. "That's

why I need your help. I need to make sure Emersyn knows what she means to me. That I'm sorry for being an idiot, but I plan to do better in the future. I want to be the man she deserves."

"Do you have a plan?"

I can see the wheels in her mind turning, trying to come up with an idea to help Emersyn and me find our happily ever after.

"I do." I smile, leaning back in the chair. "I want to throw a party."

She scrunches up her face. "How is a party going to help you make amends with Emersyn?"

"The party is just a ruse to get her there," I respond, wondering if this plan is even going to work. "She asked for me and Beckett to give her space and time to process everything that happened, and I respect that, but I don't want to go too long without begging for her forgiveness."

"Okay, I'm listening."

"Well, this is where I need your help. I know a lot about parties, but not so much about being romantic and groveling for forgiveness."

I smile, thinking back to the moment Emersyn told me she loved me. The way the moonlight reflected off her hair, casting a glow around her. The way her eyes lit up when she realized I returned her feelings, knowing for the first time that there could be something more between us.

"She told me she loved me the day before I left for deployment, but before I could tell her how I felt, Beckett came out with fire in his eyes."

"And ruined everything," Mom chimes in, her voice laced with understanding.

"I want to recreate that moment. Like a do-over, but this time, I plan to get it right."

She leans forward, cupping my cheek in her hand. "Now, *that's* a gesture."

"But how do I get her there?"

"All girls like to be swept off their feet. They want to feel special, so a *grand* gesture is in order."

"But what kind of grand gesture could say, *I fucked up for a second time, and I'm sorry. I'll probably mess up again, but I want you to know I love you and will work every day for the rest of my life to deserve you.*"

My mom smiles before pouring us both another glass. "You just leave the planning to me. I'll have the perfect setting ready for you by next week."

"Thanks, Ma. Aren't you going to give me any hints?"

"Of course, when I come up with something. All you need to worry about is how to get her to come. Leave the rest to me for now."

There are a million things she would rather be doing than be in the same place with me in front of all our friends. I doubt I can get her to come willingly, but maybe with some help from Sophie, I can at least get her to hear me out.

"All you can do is ask; the rest is up to her. But I may just have to make a call to Emersyn's mom. Between the two of us, we can make it happen."

I stand, kiss my mom on the cheek, and head out the door. I know this won't solve all our problems, but it's a step in the right direction.

I'll prove how much Emersyn Carter means to me if it's the last thing I do.

nineteen

emersyn

I slam the back door as I head inside my childhood home. I want to scream out my frustrations at the top of my lungs, but the last thing I want is to have my mother come asking questions.

"Is that you, baby girl?" my mom's voice comes from the living room.

Shit. I was hoping to at least make it to my room before I had to talk to her. I'll put money on it that Beckett called her and let her know we had a fight.

"Hey, Mama," I say in the sweetest voice, rolling my eyes at even myself.

"Did you have a chance to talk to your brother?"

"Yes, ma'am," I clip out as I turn toward the back of the house, going directly into my room and shutting the door. I toe off my shoes and flop back onto the bed, staring up at the ceiling.

"How quickly your perspective can change," I mumble to myself before tossing my arm over my eyes.

I wish that I could go back to being completely

ignorant of everyone's interference in my life. To have no idea of all the trouble my overprotective brother has caused for me. But I'm not that lucky. Instead, I get to sit here and try to figure out how to get everything I want: Brady, a happy brother, and maybe graduating with honors in a few months.

"What the fuck was he thinking?"

I sit up and storm into the bathroom and turn on the shower. "I need a shower."

It seems like an odd place to go and think, but it's my thinking space. Some people go to a therapist; I get in the shower. It's not conventional, that's for sure, but the shower is as good of a place as any to make sense of everything that has happened in the last twenty-four hours.

After reaching in to check the water temperature, I peel off my clothes and climb in. The warm water runs down my body as I step under the spray. I tilt my head back, rinsing my hair in the water, then fill my hand with shampoo and begin working it into sections of hair.

Ugh. I hate washing my hair. It just so happens that today is also wash day for my hair. Any curly-haired girl knows this is a process. When I was younger, I wore my hair as naturally as possible, adding creams and oils to keep the frizz away from curls, but recently, I've opted to keep it blown out more often now. I love my curls, don't get me wrong, but honestly, they are a lot of work and take time to maintain, something that I don't have a lot of right now. As I continue to lather, I try to make sense of everything that has happened in the last few days. I lost my virginity to my first love and had an emotional meltdown. And the pièce de résistance? Finding out that he went to my brother before talking to me.

Okay, so I turned off my phone, but he could've left a message or something. Instead, he only sent me a text message asking if I was okay. Not an apology of any sort, but somehow he thought going to see my brother would help? Fuck, men are so stupid. Even with their explanations, I'm still angry as hell.

"I can't believe how stupid he is." I turn around and wash the suds out of my hair before filling my hand with conditioner and repeating the process.

I have no idea why Beckett still feels the need to protect me from the world. He has always been there for me when I needed him, but ever since he caught me with Brady, everything has been different.

I grab the detangling brush and begin working the conditioner through my hair, taking my time to go through each section thoroughly before moving on to the next.

"What the hell is his deal?"

I have no idea, but I'm going to find out. If what I overheard in his office earlier is true, he has been actively trying to keep Brady and me apart since before

I even spoke to Brady about my feelings. Beckett has hidden behind the fact that he doesn't want me to get hurt, but there has to be something more. He needs to understand that mistakes are a fact of life. I don't need him to protect me from living. What I do need is for him to be there to comfort me when I need it.

"But Brady didn't do anything to stop it."

Right! Brady should have tried harder. He should have loved me more than anything in this world. He should have overcome anything in his way to get to me. Suddenly, a lightbulb goes off in my head, and I freeze.

He told me in his last email that he doesn't feel worthy. Why are men so stupid? They think they need to fit all these roles they assume are attractive to women, putting us on pedestals and setting expectations for themselves that are impossible for them to meet.

No one can say who deserves me except for me.

I spin around and rinse the conditioner out of my hair and then wash my body. Just as I step out of the shower and wrap a towel around my body, I hear my cell phone ring.

"It better not be one of those knuckleheads. I'm not ready to have this conversation with either of them," I growl as I bend at the hip, flipping my hair over my head and wrapping it in my microfiber towel.

My phone continues to ring loudly.

"I'm coming, I'm coming," I grumble, as if the

phone can understand me, before grabbing it and quickly answering. "What?"

I probably should have checked the caller ID to see who it was before I answered the phone that way, but I can't find it in me to care.

"Hey, chickadee," Sophie's voice chirps through the phone, entirely too happy after the copious amounts of alcohol we drank this weekend.

Sophie, Tasha, and Rachel kept me occupied all weekend, trying to make sure I didn't focus too much on what happened with Brady. Not that I've been able to think of anything but that.

"A little birdie told me you may need someone to talk to after your visit to Crawdaddy's this afternoon."

"Seriously? As if Brady hasn't done enough already." I slam my dresser drawer shut. "Or was it Beckett who called? Either way, you can tell them both to shove it."

Of course, they'd run to Sophie for help to smooth things over with me. Neither one of them has been able to deal with my being mad at them. They loathe it—have since we were kids. I should've known one or both would call her. If anyone could convince me to give him another chance, it would be Sophie. She's always been his biggest cheerleader, helping me keep faith every time he blew me off, but not this time.

"Is that so? Actually, they both called. Although, it was your brother first, but that was only because he wanted to ask if he could give Brady my phone number. Wasn't that sweet?" she coos, and I try hard not to vomit in my mouth.

I shouldn't be surprised that Beckett called Sophie. She is probably the only person in the world that could calm me down right now. Although I'm sure he just wanted another excuse to talk to her. I don't know who he thinks he's fooling, but we all know he has a thing for Sophie. Pot, meet kettle. What a hypocrite. He is determined to keep me and Brady apart, but he's doing the same thing with Sophie. Well, not exactly. I've watched those two flirt back and forth for a while, but he never makes a move. Maybe he has the same issue with himself as he has with Brady: He doesn't believe he deserves her. *What an idiot.*

"They both sounded miserable, if that helps."

"Good. They should." I pull my towel tighter around my chest. "Did you know Brady went to see Beckett today to ask for help in getting me to talk to him?"

"Wait, what?" I hear scuffling before Sophie comes back on the line. "You know what? Forget it. I'm coming cover."

I snort. "I'll have just enough time to get dressed."

"Don't get dressed on my account." She begins cackling again before hanging up the phone.

I grab a pair of yoga pants, a sports bra, and a white tank top and head back into the bathroom to get dressed. Just as I'm pulling my shirt over my head, I hear my mom calling for me.

"Emersyn!"

"In here!" I call back, pulling the towel off my hair, running leave-in conditioner through it, and adding curl cream before plopping it on the top of my head to do itself.

I'm going to have to repeat this process in about thirty minutes, but this will at least get things moving in the right direction. It's a pain in the ass to wash my hair with all these steps, but I've had years to perfect my routine. What used to take me a few hours to complete when I was younger can be done in about thirty minutes if I want to.

"Do you have plans for Friday?" My mom steps into the doorway, leaning against the doorframe and crossing her arms.

She's a little taller than me, with the same complexion. The only difference is that instead of my coils, she wears long braids down her back, the ends brushing against her waistband.

"I don't think so, but I have to check with Selina to see if she needs me to work, since she let me off for the impromptu girls' weekend."

"Oh, that won't be a problem. Debbie said everyone is invited. Seli can probably close the studio early."

I narrow my eyes at her. Something doesn't seem right about this conversation. Yes, my parents want to know where I am, but they aren't controlling. She's up to something.

"What are you up to, Mom?"

"Debbie invited us to a belated welcome-home party for Brady and his friend, Seth, next weekend. They've finally settled into civilian life, and she wants to celebrate." She steps into the room, wrapping her arm around my shoulder like she's preparing for me to fall apart. "I told her we would *all* be happy to attend."

Her extra emphasis on the word "all" can only mean one thing. She knows. The million-dollar question is, who told her, and how much of the story did they share? I have no idea who it could be, but even without specific details, I'm sure she knows something went down with Brady.

"Who told you?" I ask, panicking.

I've been trying to work through all these emotions. I thought I had time to process them. I wanted to see Brady and my brother on *my* terms, not be forced to speak to them before I was ready.

"You did. Just now." She pulls me in close and rests her cheek on the top of my head.

My eyes slide shut, relishing the feeling of being in my mom's arms.

"We've all known how much you care for Brady, baby girl. It was only a matter of time before you told him."

"I told him two years ago, but it wasn't until he

came home that I discovered how he felt about me." I brush past my mom and take a seat on my bed.

"That was brave. Not everyone has the courage to tell someone they love them." My mom takes a seat beside me and smiles.

We've always had a good relationship. If Sophie isn't available, my mom is a great ear.

"But he didn't handle things well."

"What do you mean?" she asks.

I sigh. The last thing I want to tell my mom is that I lost my virginity and that he ran away from me again on the same day. But how is she going to help if I don't tell her everything?

"We slept together, and he ran away from me."

"Oh! I wasn't expecting that." She recoils slightly, placing her hand over her chest.

"Neither was I." I snicker, sure that this is just as startling to her as it was to me when it happened.

"Baby girl, I'm going to let you in on a secret. Something you will learn the more interaction you have with the male species."

"They're idiots," I mutter.

"So, you knew."

We both laugh as she grips my hand, giving it a squeeze.

"It takes them time to catch up to us sometimes. Women know how to deal with their feelings, but men often don't know what to do with theirs. They need some more time to process and think things through."

"I should forgive him just like that?" I stand and begin pacing. "How will I know he won't do it again?"

"You won't. And I didn't say that, but maybe cut him some slack."

"Honey, I'm home!" Sophie barges into my bedroom. "Oh, sorry. Mr. Carter let me in on his way out."

My mom smiles at her before standing and giving me a hug. "Just think about it, baby girl. You don't want to have any regrets."

She waves at Sophie before heading out of the room.

"What'd I miss?" she asks.

"Brady's having a party in a few days, and I'm invited."

"Well, shit."

"My sentiments exactly," I concur.

twenty

emersyn

Today is the day: the infamous day of Brady's party. I've tried everything to get out of this party, but my mom hasn't budged. She reminded me that the Thomases have been close friends of ours for my entire life and said the least I could do was attend a party in Brady and Seth's honor. Talk about a major guilt trip.

"We're headed out, Em. Sophie just pulled up in front of the house." My mom smiles before coming into my room and giving me a hug. "Everything is going to work out as it should."

"How can you be sure?"

"Just call it mother's intuition." She winks at me, then turns and heads out the door.

If anyone would have asked me if I thought I would be sitting on the edge of my bed tonight, waiting to see if the man I love will man up and tell me how he feels for the third time, I'd have called them insane.

I still have no idea what to do about Brady or

Beckett. Thankfully, neither of them has tried to contact me. Beckett was here during the week, but he kept his distance. I'm sure my parents know something is up between the two of us, but neither one of them has said anything. I was sure he would try to get them on his side or get them to force me to speak to him at the very least. But for the first time in my life, he's respected my choices. One crisis averted.

I've debated calling Brady every day this week to try to talk things over, but I just couldn't bring myself to do it. Hell, I don't even know how I'm feeling about everything myself. On the one hand, I understand his hesitation to get involved with me. It must be hard to basically start your life over at thirty-eight. He went from having a steady career with decent pay to having to work in an entirely different trade. Moving home couldn't have been easy either. While I'm planning on graduating in a few months, getting a place of my own, and maybe even starting a design business, Brady is back living with his parents. That must do something to a man's self-esteem.

"Ready to get out of here?" Sophie strides into my room and flops down on my bed.

I give her a forced smile as I walk into my closet and grab my favorite pair of Chuck Taylors.

"That's what you're wearing?" she scoffs, pushing up off the bed and heading toward me. "This won't do at all. The least you can do is *pretend* you want to be at the party."

"But I don't," I deadpan, looking down at my dark-washed boyfriend jeans with strategically placed rips down the legs and the dark purple Chucks in my hand.

I put on my favorite oversized gray sweater, hanging it strategically off my left shoulder, leaving just enough to the imagination. My hair is in its usual curly mess on my head, pushed into a bun with a deep purple scarf.

"At least I put on some makeup."

I would point to my face, but Sophie is still searching my closet. I didn't do anything fancy. Just some eyeliner, mascara, and a little lip gloss, which is a lot for me.

Sophie thrusts a bohemian peasant top at me. "Put this on. I'll find you some shoes to match because you are not wearing those old Chucks."

"But I love my Chucks," I pout, pulling my sweater over my head and replacing it with the top she chose for me.

I do have to admit this is much more flattering than my original choice. The off-white lightweight material hangs off both my shoulders, exposing a little more skin than I'd like, but it isn't inappropriate at all. An arrangement of red, purple, and orange flowers runs down the center of the shirt.

"I don't hate it," I announce, heading over to the full-length mirror in the corner of the room.

"Of course, you don't." She smirks, placing a pair of hoop earrings in my hand and dropping a pair of peep-toe black wedge sandals in front of me on the floor. "He won't know what hit him, girl."

"Whatever you say." I turn from side to side in the mirror. "At least he'll know what he's missing when he sees me."

"You decided to kick him to the curb." Sophie lowers her voice.

I know she doesn't want to sway my decision either way, but I also know whose side she's on. She has been Team Brady since day one, always talking me off the ledge when I'm ready to throw in the towel. But this time, even she has to admit how badly he messed up.

"I don't know, honestly. I know he hurt me, but I kind of understand where he was coming from. Then add the bullshit with my brother into the mix, and everything gets even more complicated." I thread the posts of each earring through my ears before bending over to grab the shoes.

"That's fair. But can you promise me one thing?" Sophie grips my elbow, pulling me to a stop.

"This sounds serious."

"Can you just hear him out? I know he hurt you, but keep an open mind, okay? If you don't like what he has to say, we can leave. We'll call the girls and get completely wasted again."

My only worry in all of this is that Brady is still afraid of losing my brother as a friend, not being good enough, or whatever else is going on in his head that's keeping him from taking the leap with me.

"I've laid my heart on the line for him twice now. I don't know if I want to do it a third time."

"I understand that, but you can't expect him to take a leap of faith without you doing the same thing."

"Okay, I'll at least hear him out. But I can't make any promises about anything else."

"Just the answer I wanted to hear." A wide smile spreads across her face as she reaches over the side of the bed and grabs her bag.

"What are you looking for? We're getting ready to leave. Can't it wait?" I ask, leaning to the side, hoping to get a glimpse of what she's searching for.

"Here." Sophie holds out a small white envelope. "Brady was afraid you wouldn't talk to him at the party, but he wanted to make sure you knew how he felt."

I tentatively take the envelope from her and hold it at arm's length.

"It's not a bomb. Just a letter from the man you love."

"Do you know what he wrote?" I ask, hoping for a hint.

She shakes her head and pushes off the bed. "I have

no idea. Whatever is inside that envelope is for you and only you. I'm going to be in the living room. Just come out when you're ready."

Emersyn,

I know I've been responding to you via email, but since this is a special occasion, I figured the old-fashioned way would be best. I fucked up again. I know that, and I know I'll fuck up again in the future, but all I can do is ask for your forgiveness.

I told you in my last email that I was insecure, but that's only the tip of the iceberg. Insecure is an understatement; downright terrified is more like it. Growing up, I always felt like I was playing catch-up. Like everyone had this perfect plan for their lives, and I just floated along through life with no purpose. When I graduated from high school, it got worse. All my friends were moving on to bigger and better things, making their way in the world, but I was standing still. I joined the Marines, hoping that would give me a purpose, something to work toward, but it did the opposite. I had someone telling me what to do every day, what to eat, and how to act. So instead of growing into something more than I was, I was stuck. All those voices telling me I wasn't good enough only became louder. I thought I had them under control, that I could ignore them, but they just got louder.

I know I've said this a million times, but I'm going to say it once more for good measure. I love you. I honestly can't say when it started, but it has grown every day, turning into an all-encompassing passion that sets my heart on fire. I always seem to ruin things when I try to tell you how I feel. I'd like to make excuses for my actions, but there's only one: fear.

I was afraid that everything the voices in my head were saying to me was true. That I would ruin your life. That I'd never be the man you believed I was, the man you deserve to have by your side. But I'm through letting fear rule my life. You have come to mean more to me than anything else in this world. Just one look from you, *and I know that no matter what happens, I have you in my corner.*

It's not Beckett's fault. He was doing what he thought was best for you and protecting you in the only way he knew how. He and I have the same fear. The fear that one day you will wake up and regret your decision to be with me.

I wanted to make a grand gesture and show you in front of all our friends and family that you're it for me, but when I thought about it, I knew that wasn't your style. So instead, I chose to write you a letter. A letter that's way overdue.

I promise to love you for the rest of my life and to strive to become the man that you see when you look at me. A man who will spend the rest of his life trying to deserve the precious gift you have given him: your heart.

Love you always,
Brady

P.S. If there's even a chance of you giving me another chance, meet me in my parents' backyard for the surprise of your life. I'll be there waiting for you when you're ready.

Lines of mascara stream down my face as I finish his letter. He was right. There was no way I would have been comfortable with a big production. Those are more for other people than the person involved. This is better. A letter, something I've been waiting to get from him since he left on deployment. A few simple paragraphs letting me know exactly how he feels about me.

The fact that he was able to realize this after everything we've been through speaks volumes. Brady knows me in a way no one else does or ever will.

I couldn't have asked for anything more.

"Finished?" Sophie knocks on the door twice. "I know I said I would wait in the living room, but I'm impatient."

I giggle softly. "I didn't really think you would. I'm actually surprised you lasted this long. I expected to look up from the letter and see you sitting in front of me."

"I was tempted, but I knew this was something you needed to do alone."

"You're right. Thank you."

I fold the letter, put it back in the envelope, and

place it on my bedside table. I'm going to cherish this note for the rest of my life.

"For what?" she asks.

If it wasn't for my meddling best friend, I doubt I'd have any idea of how Brady felt about me. I would still be sitting here, wrapped in my indecision.

"For always being Team Brady." I stand, walk over to my best friend, and give her a big hug.

She hugs me back tightly before we break apart.

"You were right. I was ready to give up on the best thing that ever happened to me."

Sophie fist pumps the air before trying to play it off by running her hands through her hair. "So, what now?"

"Now we head over to that party so I can give him my answer." I thread my arm through hers and smile.

"I like the sound of that."

twenty-one

brady

"You need to chill out, Brady." Beckett slaps me on the back before handing me another beer.

"Are you sure she's coming?" I grab the beer from his hand and continue pacing in front of the picture window in my parents' living room.

The last week has been torture, not being able to contact Emersyn, but I wanted to respect her wishes. That was the least I could do after everything I put her through. It also gave Beckett and me time to talk and work things out and for him to articulate to me what his issue was.

It wasn't that he didn't want Emersyn and me to be together, but he saw how much she cared for me. He was afraid that she would be like so many girls and lose who she was. Mold herself into anything I wanted. When she announced to the family a few nights before my going away party that she planned on staying in town and commuting to school, he saw that as the beginning of the change. So, instead of supporting his sister in her decision, he convinced her that she wanted her independence. She was only going to school a couple hours' drive away, and there were plenty of apartments for her to rent once she knew the area better.

I laughed my ass off for a full hour when he said that. I could never imagine a world where Emersyn was anything but herself. Besides, she has Sophie. If Sophie had noticed that kind of change in her friend, it would have been nipped in the bud immediately.

Beckett and I have patched things up for the most part. I'm not going to say things are back to normal, but I'm glad to have my friend back.

"Did you give Sophie my letter?"

Beckett rolls his eyes at me for the millionth time today. "Yes, and before you ask, she promised to make sure Em opened it."

Knowing Emersyn, she's a bundle of nerves, just like me, ready to burst at any moment. That's one of the main reasons I chose to write her a letter instead of putting her on the spot here in front of everyone. There's no way to let someone down easily with all your family watching them crash and burn. Then get our two mothers involved, and it could turn into a disaster. I doubt either one of them would have let Emersyn out this door with any other answer than yes.

"They're here," Beckett mumbles, pointing his beer out the window.

My eyes pan to the right, finally seeing Emersyn for the first time in a week. My heart begins pounding in my chest, the sound ringing in my ears as I step toward the front door.

"Aren't you going to wait for her to come inside?" he asks, gripping my shoulder to hold me in place.

I shrug his hand off. "I'm not waiting another minute to tell her face-to-face what she means to me."

He smiles, stepping out of my way. "Go get her, tiger. But remember, if you hurt her, I know how to hide a body."

I give him a mock salute before flinging the door open and striding toward her. Our eyes lock, and she smiles, lighting up my life for the first time in weeks.

My vision blurs, and I can see nothing else but her. The way the sun reflects off her curls shows the flecks of red and gold that only come out when she has too much sun. I can see the flecks of green in her honey-brown eyes. Eyes that hold nothing but love and devotion as she stares into mine.

I stop in front of her, wanting to pull her into my arms, but resist. I need to hear her answer, but first I need to apologize for everything I've done wrong.

"I'm sorry," we both say at the same time, before breaking into nervous laughter.

"What do you have to be sorry for?" I ask, grabbing

both of her hands in mine. "You are the kindest and most understanding person on the face of this earth. Any other woman would have told me to kick rocks by now, but not you."

"I'm sorry for making you feel like you were anything less than amazing." Emersyn steps forward, wrapping her arms around my neck.

"Baby, that wasn't the case at all. It's because of you that I feel like I can do anything."

Without hesitation, Emersyn slams her lips on mine. I groan loudly, wrapping my arms around her tightly before sliding my tongue into her mouth. There is no fight for domination, just relief. Relief to finally have everything I've ever wanted right here in my arms.

"God, you two, get a room!"

We break apart, gasping for air, as Sophie snaps a picture with her phone.

"Sorry. I couldn't resist," she chuckles.

Emersyn buries her nose into my chest as I laugh loudly. "You're forgiven. Under two conditions."

"Name it." Sophie hides her phone behind her back, ready to run from us if she needs to.

"First, you text me that picture."

Sophie nods her head in agreement, and my phone pings in my pocket, signaling an incoming text.

"That one's easy. And the second?"

I look down at Emersyn and plant a kiss on her forehead. "Go keep Beckett from coming out here and ripping my head off. We may have buried the hatchet, but I don't think he's going to take kindly to me having my hands all over his little sister."

"I happen to agree. Besides, annoying Beckett is my favorite pastime." Sophie smiles and heads toward the front door.

"When is my brother going to give in? We all know how much he likes her." Emersyn smiles up at me.

"I think he may be coming around." I grip her chin, tilting it upwards. "We may be talking him off the same ledge I was just on."

Emersyn giggles, nipping at my thumb as I brush it against her lips. "I love you."

"I know," I respond, brushing my lips against hers.

"What, are we in a *Star Wars* movie?" She rises onto her toes slightly, licking the seam between my lips with the tip of her tongue.

"I've always had a thing for the princess. Besides, the movie has nothing on you." Unable to resist any longer, I lean down and kiss her.

"Brady," she says breathlessly, before gripping the back of my neck and pulling me in for a deep kiss.

I'm caught by surprise at first but soon lean my body into hers.

She drags her lips up the left side of my face to whisper in my ear. "Can we have a do-over?"

I pull back slightly, a devious grin spreading across

my face. "You think we could make it up to my apartment without anyone noticing?"

"Sophie is occupying Beckett, so no one knows I've gotten here but you."

Without a word, I bend down and flip her over my shoulder before making a beeline for the stairs to my apartment. I take them two at a time, sending up a silent prayer of thanks for Seth being occupied downstairs and that he moved into his new place a few weeks ago. I love the guy like a brother, but I need to have this time with my girl. A chance to erase all the bad memories of our first time together.

I make it to the top in record time, opening the door with one hand before lowering her to her feet. "This is it. No going back."

"I love you," she whispers before pressing her body into mine.

"I love you." I put my arm under her knees, carrying her inside before kicking the door shut behind me.

She trails light kisses down my neck as I enter my bedroom and lay her down softly on the bed.

"This is our first time together," I tell her. "I want to make you forget anything before today."

"A new beginning." She smiles as I lean down, pressing her body into the bed with mine.

I reach down and grab the bottom of her shirt, dragging it up. "This is in my fucking way." Then I lean down and brush gentle kisses on her skin, circling her belly button with my tongue. "Lift up for me. I want to feast on all of you."

Emersyn wastes no time arching her back as I inch her shirt higher, exposing more skin. I pull her shirt up and over her head, but instead of pulling it off, I use it to secure her hands.

"Don't want you trying to get away from me." I give her a wink before slinking back down her body.

I continue to nip and suck at the sensitive skin of her stomach, using my right hand to massage her tit through her bra. I look up, seeing nothing but desire in her eyes, and flip open the button of her jeans, pulling them down. She lifts her hips and helps lower her pants and panties before kicking them off onto the floor.

"That always looks sexier in the movies, but in reality, it's hard and awkward as fuck to do." She giggles as she lies back, spreading her legs wide. "Now, can you get back to it?"

I've always loved how she knows what she wants. Never demands but is never shy about it either. Without a word, I suck her clit deep into my mouth while easing my middle finger into her folds, her walls tightening around me.

"Nothing will ever taste as good as you for as long as I live," I mumble as I bury my face deeper, lapping her juices as they drip from inside her.

"Oh, Brady. I need more!" She reaches down, gripping my hair in her hands and pulling, sending ripples of pain mixed with pleasure down my spine.

I grind my hips into the bed, searching for needed relief.

"Careful, baby. You'll make me come like a teenager if you keep that up." I nip at the inside of her left leg as I insert another finger, continuing to pump them in and out.

She arches her back, screaming my name as I find that bundle of nerves again, bringing her closer to the edge.

"You want my cock now, don't you? You want me inside you, fucking the shit out of this pussy," I growl before attacking her clit and sucking hard, sending her over the edge into oblivion.

I drag my fingers from her pussy, then crawl up her body and grind my rock-hard cock against her core as I take possession of her mouth.

I rock back and forth, rubbing my still-covered cock between her folds and not-so-accidentally hitting her engorged clit in the process.

"Stop teasing me, damn it!" she whines as she reaches for the button on my jeans.

Quickly, I finish what she started and discard the rest of my clothes.

"So impatient." I insert the tip inside her, just enough for us both to ache for more.

This is torture, but watching her squirm is like a

drug. Knowing I'm the one that is giving her this pleasure and that she hasn't had it like this from anyone but me is my personal aphrodisiac.

"Please," she begs, sitting up and wrapping her arms and legs around me. "I need you."

There is a fire in her eyes that wasn't there before, one that tells me she needs this as much as I do.

"Your wish is my command." Gripping her under the ass, I thrust forward and sheath myself inside her.

I try to take my time, to make this more than just fucking, but my need to claim her—mind, body, and soul—is overwhelming.

"I love you," I whisper in reverence as I pump in and out of her.

"Yes! Yes! Brady!" Emersyn rakes her fingers down my back before wrapping her legs around me, pulling me closer and meeting me thrust for thrust.

Our pace quickens as I thrust harder into her core, and I grit my teeth together as I try to hold off my release. Emersyn's eyes meet mine as her walls begin to tighten, signaling her impending orgasm.

I snake my hand between our bodies, pinching her clit between my fingers.

"Come for me, baby," I whisper as I pull her earlobe into my mouth, biting down hard.

My hips continue to slap against hers until she shouts my name, and both of us tumble over the edge.

I lean forward so our foreheads are touching and smile. "Better than the first time?"

"Not really. I don't have much else to compare it to." She brushes a gentle kiss on my lips.

I snort. "I guess I'll have to work harder next time."

"Are you sure you're up for it, old man?" she teases, but it turns into a gasp as I thrust forward again, nowhere close to satisfied.

"What can I say? I have good stamina."

"I love you."

The sparkle in her eyes as she utters those three magical words says it all. I have the only thing I have ever wanted in life: her heart.

"I love you more." I capture her mouth in a kiss and give myself over to the passion I felt for the woman I was afraid I'd lost forever.

We may have had a rocky start and a dysfunctional beginning, but we ended up with a happy ending. People may say we know nothing about each other, or that she's just beginning her life while I'm on a downward descent, but none of those things matter. What matters is the love we have for each other and the desire to grow together as one, pushing each other to be better people with each passing day.

Life won't always be perfect for me and Emersyn. I know there will be ups and downs, but we're going to have a hell of a lot of fun along the way.

epilogue

emersyn

eighteen months later

"Bye, Ms. Emersyn!" Carolina and Hailey shout as they head to the cubbies and grab their things.

I've been teaching at Selina's studio full time since before I graduated a little over a year ago. I don't have nearly as much free time as I did before, but I seem to make it work. It helps that my boss also happens to be friends with my boyfriend. The perks of having an older man on your arm.

"Bye, girls." I follow them and their mother to the door, locking it behind them. "Finally."

I tilt my head toward the ceiling, the back of my head thumping on the door.

I was supposed to have the day off today, but when Selina called, begging me to come in and teach her classes, I couldn't say no.

Today is the day we've all been waiting for. Seth and Bristol are getting engaged. As if there's a chance that she'll say anything but yes. Those two are more in love than anyone I know, expect maybe my parents. Oh, and me and Brady.

Although we had a rocky start, every day we have spent together has been better than the last, just as Brady promised me all that time ago.

"Knock, knock."

I spin around and smile when I see Brady's smiling face on the other side of the glass.

"I come bearing gifts." He holds up two bags of food from our favorite restaurant.

"I don't know." I tap the end of my chin, pretending to think. "Got anything else in there?"

He snickers as I unlock the door and pull it open. "How about a kiss?"

"Hmmm, I think that helps, but still, I don't know. My boss hates it when I let people in after hours."

Brady pushes his way through the door, pinning me to the wall.

"I can think of other things your boss wouldn't like you doing while you're here." He chuckles darkly before smashing his lips to mine.

A shiver runs down my entire body as he nibbles on my bottom lip, and I open my mouth, massaging his tongue with mine, gripping the hairs at the back of his neck.

Brady groans loudly, stepping out of my embrace. "Don't start something you aren't ready to finish."

"How about we forget about the food and you have

me instead?" I peck him on the lips quickly before scurrying down the hallway toward the reception area.

He groans again, smacking me hard on the ass before I make it around the desk and out of his reach.

"Promises, promises," I tease.

He chuckles before dropping down into one of the chairs and crossing his legs.

Today is mine and Brady's anniversary. Not a major one, but Brady insists on making a big deal out of it. I was a little skeptical about going along with his plans, but when he told me we would be spending a long weekend in a secluded bungalow down at Seaside Cove, who was I to turn him down?

"I just need to turn off the lights and make sure the back door is locked, and we can go," I say just as my phone chimes. "I wonder who that is."

I pause, reaching into a drawer to pull out my phone.

"Did you get a text from Selina, too?" Brady slides his phone across the counter toward me.

I find a picture of Bristol and Seth standing in the middle of a sunflower field surrounded by everyone, and Selina's face popping out of the corner.

SELINA

SHE SAID YES!

I snort as I hand the phone back to him. "Of course, she said yes. Did he have any doubt?"

"You never know with you ladies. Some of you like the plans and grand gestures, and some of you just want to be alone with the man you love." He smiles as he slides his phone back into his pocket. "Which would you prefer?"

"Honestly, it doesn't matter. You down on one knee. A ring. I'm not picky."

I turn and head toward the back, taking my time as I check all the doors and turn off all the lights in the dance rooms.

"Aren't you going to change?" he asks.

"I'm going to be naked in a few minutes anyway. What's the point of changing?" I say, shutting off the lights and heading toward the front of the studio.

As I round the corner, I gasp in surprise.

"Based on your answer, now is as good of a time as any." Brady smirks, down on one knee and a shining princess-cut diamond set in a white gold band clasped between his fingers. "I had this whole speech planned. We would be on the beach at sunset after spending the day hanging out, maybe have a picnic on the beach for dinner with a bonfire crackling in the background. I would have waited for the grand finale, and then I would have dropped to one knee and professed my undying love for you."

Tears pool in my eyes as I contemplate what my life would have been like if I hadn't taken a leap of faith and believed that Brady wouldn't run again.

"That does sound like an amazing plan," I whisper, stepping toward him. "What made you change your mind?"

He chuckles, his cheeks darkening. "Honestly, I couldn't wait another moment to make you my wife."

"Well, since you asked so nicely..."

A huge smile spreads across his face as he slides the ring onto my finger before standing to his full height and lifting me in the air. We spin in circles as if we're the only two people in the world, and right now, we are.

"Thank you," Brady whispers before lowering me down to the floor and kissing the top of my head.

"I should be thanking you."

"How about we call it even?" He chuckles.

"I can live with that," I say with a smile.

the end

I hope you enjoyed *Love You Always*! Wondering what happened to Brady and Emersyn after the end? Scan the QR code for instant access to a bonus epilogue for your new favorite couple.

Already subscribed? Just check your last newsletter for the link to my bonus material! If you can't find it, you can simply resubscribe and the scene will be yours in minutes!

USA Today Bestselling Author AJ Alexander has been writing romance since 2018. She loves writing small town romances with found families and all the nosey nellies that help her characters find their happily ever afters! She lives in Arizona, otherwise known as the surface of the sun, with her husband, two daughters, two cats, and a lovable golden retriever.

When she isn't writing you can find AJ reading, binging the latest true crime documentary on Netflix, or binging the latest Korean Drama or Anime that's released. AJ is a cynical hopeless romantic that believes in love at first sight, that bigger is always better, and everything should be put off for a nap.

Come find her in the wild! There's nothing she loves more than connecting with my readers.

www.ingramcontent.com/pod-product-compliance
Lightning Source LLC
LaVergne TN
LVHW100517110826
845146LV00002B/676

* 9 7 9 8 9 8 9 8 2 5 0 7 3 *